The Australian Pen – Volume 3

The Evil Inside Us

First printing, 2018

0 1 2 3 4 5 6 7 8 9

Paperback ISBN: 978-0-6481979-2-8
Digital ISBN: 978-0-6481979-3-5

1231 Publishing
PO Box 77
Kallangur QLD 4503
Australia

Contents

SPIDERWEBS

Sophie L Macdonald

A crown of bright red hair, swirling in the water. It looked like an orange starburst in a brown sky. Then the screaming started.

'Charlie!' That was the mother—all nails and teeth and howls. Amazing how we become animals again when something threatens our young.

They held her back. She was no longer human, and the sounds she was making vibrated through all of our bones as if we were one person. We felt her.

Then time sped up again. The men jumped in and dragged him out, and all of a sudden it was a little boy—blue and lifeless, hair flat against his skin. They pressed his chest, and called for help, but anyone could see it was too late.

I saw it all.

The other one, a local boy, clung to his father.

Reverend Pete—he was all of our fathers every Sunday—cradled his son's head as if to shield him from what he'd already seen.

'What happened, Sammy?' The Reverend was white around the mouth—nothing like the calm man who prayed for our loved ones and splashed water on the heads of our newborns.

'I don't know, Daddy.' Sam's eyes were wide—darting between his father's face and the body of the boy on the ground. His trousers were wet at the ends. 'I tried to wade in to save him, but I was scared of the water.'

I wanted to tell those men to stop bothering at the body. That boy was in Heaven.

'We were just playing. I didn't even see him fall in.'

The dam was still. When my children were young we went there to throw crusts for the ducks. You're not supposed to do that—the bread can kill them. Everyone knows they shouldn't now, but people still do it. The birds like it, and I'm sure the odd piece can't hurt.

That brown circle of water is like the bullseye of our village. At Christmas, the Reverend's church holds Carols by the Lake there. It's not really a lake though.

It didn't look inviting right at that moment. It looked to me like something that could suck you under forever. I was reminded of being in the bath as a child, and scrambling to get out before the plug got removed.

The paramedics couldn't do anything, and Charlie had a sheet over his head before they even put him on the stretcher.

His mother was the one getting all the attention. The father was just staring at the spot on the ground where they pulled Charlie out. His clothes were wet, but no one brought him a blanket.

'Weren't you watching them?' Mary, the Reverend's wife, was pulling at his arm. 'That could have been Sam in there. They're only six. They can't be trusted near the water.'

'I was watching them,' Pete said.

'How could he fall in?' Mary asked. 'Did you see?'

The conversation seemed to hang there for a moment, as we all looked at the Reverend. A moment in time when a community's heart beats as one.

'Did anyone see what happened?' A policeman broke through the silence.

'I didn't see,' we all said.

We don't get new families in our village often. There's no industry that brings anyone here. People leave all the time for bigger things and brighter lights. Most of the families have been here forever one way or another though. It's like we're made up of long silvery spiderwebs that reach back in time, all tied together at different points. Bits break off now and again, but we're all part of the same web.

Reverend Pete's father was the priest before him, and I expect little Sammy will grow up in his father's footsteps. The church is the heart of the village, and it beats through all our veins. There are those who don't believe, and that's okay, but if you want to be a part of things then you go to the Carols by the Lake, and the Easter egg hunt, and the barbeque to welcome a new family member to the village.

Suzanne and Michael, Charlie's parents, were the first outsiders to move here in a long time. I don't mean to be rude by calling them outsiders—we love new people—it just doesn't happen very often.

Of course, the church put on a barbeque by the dam to welcome them. Charlie was the same age as Pete and Mary's little boy, Sam, and he would be going to the local school.

No one could have known this would happen.

A policeman moved around taking statements from people, and he said he might need to call us in for proper interviews. I knew him—it was Jeremy Williams. I went to school with his mum. I used to babysit him sometimes.

'Hi, Mrs Albeck,' he nodded his head at me. 'Bloody awful thing to happen. Did you see how he fell?'

I looked him straight in the eye. 'I didn't see anything,' I said. 'His poor mum and dad.'

'Yes, terrible,' he agreed and then, because it was just me and him, he quietly added: 'Thank God it wasn't a local.'

I nodded agreement, glancing at the boy's

mother and father. That's not to say it was any better because he was an outsider, of course, but we didn't know the family. There would not be the same grief there would be for a child I had cradled in hospital, or one who sold me Scout cookies or raffle tickets outside the supermarket or, Heaven forbid, little Sammy himself.

'Just so you know,' Jeremy leant in, 'the mum's making some kind of accusation. She's saying she saw Sam push her boy in the dam.' He put a hand on my arm. 'Don't worry, though. We can all see she's in a lot of shock at the moment, and that will be the grief talking.'

'Is your dad here?' I asked. Jeremy's dad was our local police chief. I thought I had seen him drinking a beer by the barbeque earlier.

'Yes, he's with the mum now,' Jeremy said. 'Dad didn't see him fall in, but he was keeping an eye on them, and Sam was nowhere near him at the time.'

I looked across, and saw Charlie's mother screaming and waving her arms around—pointing at Sam, who clung to his father's leg.

'Someone should get Sam out of here,' I said. 'He shouldn't have to see all of this. He's only six.'

'I'll talk to Pete.' Jeremy went to talk to the Reverend. From there, the party began to disperse, and we were all encouraged to go home and let the police contact us if they needed to.

It's not as if any of us would be hard to find.

The following day I went to find the Reverend at church. I'd hoped he would be alone, but Sam was helping him set up the bibles and kneeling mats ready for the next service.

'How is he?' I spoke quietly, indicating to Sam.

'He's taking it hard,' Pete said. 'I'm hoping the service will help. I want to bring everyone together—focus on supporting the parents and each other. Hopefully we can all move away from blame.'

'I didn't do it.' Sam's face was solemn; his soft brown eyes staring into mine. 'You know I didn't push him, Mrs Albeck.'

'Of course you didn't,' I agreed. 'People say funny things when they're sad. They get confused.'

'Will I go to jail?' Sam's eyes were shiny with the threat of tears.

'No!' Pete kneeled next to him. 'You have done nothing wrong, Sammy. I know it, the police know it, and God knows it. Charlie's mummy was just very upset, and we have to help her see it was an accident—nothing to do with you.'

'What if she doesn't believe us?' Sam said.

'Then it doesn't matter,' I answered sharply, 'because the head of the police was right there, and he saw everything. He saw that you were nowhere near Charlie,' I said.

Sam flung himself at me and gave me a hug. He flashed a big smile.

'Thank you, Mrs Albeck!' he said.

Pete smiled and stroked his hair.

'Thanks, Sharon,' he said. 'It's times like this when a community needs to support each other.'

He turned to take some candles out the back, and Sam pulled back a little.

'You were watching us,' he said quietly.

I didn't answer.

'I didn't mean to hurt him,' he continued. 'I just wanted to know what he would look like if he was blue.'

Sam's eyes were fixed on mine, and I flashed back to holding him in my arms when he was a baby. Mary had struggled as a new mum, and we'd all taken our turns to help her out—feeding him, rocking him to sleep. It's what you do for each other.

'Of course you didn't hurt him,' I said quickly. 'Put that thought out of your head. You didn't do anything wrong.'

I bumped into Suzanne outside the church. When I'd first seen her I thought she looked too glamorous for the village. She was all highlights and shiny make-up. I'd laughed to myself about how long that would last when she realised there were no big department stores here and no one to impress with that sort of nonsense. She didn't look like that now. She looked grey.

'How are you doing, love?' I asked. She seemed confused, so I prompted her. 'It's Sharon Albeck. The Reverend introduced us before.' I didn't have to explain what I meant by 'before'.

'Oh, Sharon, yes.' She blinked as if she couldn't focus, and then suddenly seized my arm. 'You were there. Did you see what he did? The police don't believe me, but I saw it happen—I just couldn't get there in time.'

'No, I'm sorry,' I said. 'I didn't see.'

'How can it be that no one saw a bloody thing?' Her voice was too loud. 'Why are you all trying to protect that kid? We went to their house when we first arrived, and Charlie told me that boy was burning ants with his magnifying glass.'

'All boys do that.' I glanced at the church door, hoping Sam and Reverend Pete couldn't hear this.

'He told Charlie that he'd killed his own cat,' she spat the words out. 'He said he'd drowned her in the bath, just to see what she looked like when she was dead. He buried her body in the backyard. I told Charlie he was probably lying to impress him, but I didn't want him having anything to do with that little psycho.' She swiped at the tears on her face.

'Oh, that's ridiculous,' I said, but I was thinking of the time Sam's cat, Minky, had gone missing. We had prayed for her safe return in church, whilst Sam wiped tears from his eyes, just like Suzanne was doing then.

I reached out to her. 'We're having a service in the morning. Will you come? Everyone wants to help you if we can.'

'You can help by telling the truth to the police,' she said, 'or by standing up in that bloody service and telling everyone what you saw.' Her face was close to mine now, and I wondered how I had ever thought she was glamorous. 'He held his foot on my son's head when he was underwater.'

'Everything happened so fast,' I said. The sun was hot on my face, and I started to feel dizzy. 'It was hard to tell what was going on with all the commotion.'

'You're just as bad as he is,' she hissed the words, and wrenched the door of the church open, leaving me standing alone feeling a bit sick.

I hoped Sam wasn't there to hear whatever she said to the Reverend.

The whole village gathered for the service the next morning. Poor Charlie's body was still with the coroner, so his funeral wouldn't be for a few more days. This service was to unite us after the tragedy that had happened at our centre. I could see Suzanne and Michael from across the aisle, and I was glad they had come.

Reverend Pete greeted us, with Sam at his side—looking small and pale in a little suit. In fifteen years that boy would be dressed like his father, leading us all.

The heat was getting too much, and I fidgeted in my seat as the Reverend spoke of community and togetherness.

A howl broke through the Reverend's sermon, and we all turned to look at Suzanne.

'This is such bullshit!' she shouted, as Michael tried to pull her down. 'Almost every single one of you saw what happened!' She pointed at Jeremy's father—the police chief. 'You of all people should tell the truth. And you!' She turned to face

Reverend Pete. 'A man of God, and you stand in His house telling lies! You don't need unity: you are already bound together in your lies!'

She looked at each of us in turn. 'Won't one person stand up and tell the truth about what you saw? Tell the truth before God.'

I stood up. I didn't know what I was going to say, and my knees were shaking. She was right. We were in God's house, and no one was telling the truth.

Sam stared hard at me, and I pictured him burning ants and drowning his cat—drowning Charlie. This boy would be our leader.

Everyone was staring at me. I opened my mouth.

'I didn't see anything.' The words fell out like jagged little spikes, and I knew Suzanne felt them.

Jeremy stood too. 'I didn't see anything,' he said.

One by one, everyone stood, until we were all standing with Reverend Pete and Sam, repeating those words.

'I didn't see anything.'

Suzanne gave a sob and ran from the church, Michael at her heels, and we all stood silently looking to Reverend Pete for guidance.

'Let us not judge Suzanne and Michael,' he began, 'for we know they are in pain. Sometimes we sin. Sometimes we make mistakes. Accidents happen.' His eyes met mine. 'But we will not judge each other by our mistakes. We will forgive and we will support one another, as we have done for hundreds of years. Let us pray now, together.'

We closed our eyes. After a moment I opened mine, to see Sam looking at me. He gave me a thumbs up. I closed my eyes, and in my prayer I imagined a silver thread of our love for each other winding around us all. For a moment an image flashed into my mind of a spiderweb, with us stuck around the edges, bound in silver cocoons, and Sam sitting fatly in the middle, awaiting his meal. Then it was gone, and I felt the peace and love of our community again.

PLEASED TO MEET YOU

Linda Conlon

The first time he saw her, he knew. She didn't notice him and certainly had no idea he was standing there planning Their Future. She stood behind the counter, speaking to another customer, laughing and smiling. He was transfixed by her riotous hair, held in a precarious auburn knot atop her head and the ringlets that had escaped capture, coiled like tiny dragons about her nape. He was intoxicated by the curve of her plump lips; the way they curled as they shared a secretive joke or compressed disapprovingly when her manager yelled a question at her, interrupting her easy conversation. He was dazzled by her eyes, adrift in their blue twinkle and enraptured by the notion that he'd finally found the harbour he hadn't known he needed.

When it was his turn to order, he was as

charming as he knew how to be and he thrummed with her returned favour, knowing deep inside that she felt it, too.

Their first date was fun and romantic, the night passing in a whirl of colour and laughter so heartfelt there were snorts. She was embarrassed, he was captivated. Their second date was held the next night because they were already craving each other. It was an even greater success but their third date took an unexpected turn to seriousness when his mother had a fall and was taken to hospital. They were both from large families so she parried his tribe's friendly interrogations with aplomb and just the right amount of sass. By the time his mother was released with a cast and a serving of wounded pride, his whole family had taken her in and decided she was one of their own.

She had never been happier. He was so perfect, she couldn't have dreamt a better match for herself.

He was absorbed just as efficiently by her family and no-one was surprised when they announced their engagement after just six months. She and her girlfriends got together to plan a charming engagement party followed by gregarious bachelor and hens' nights and, at last, the wedding. Everyone agreed they were a fairytale couple, sickeningly in love and destined to be the envy of their circle forever. The word 'magical' was used so often at the reception that it became a running joke. Still, guests were at a loss to come up with a better descriptor.

After the wedding, life continued at a cracking pace. New jobs, promotions, the first home, the sale of the first home, breaking ground on the first built home, new cars, new hobbies, new pets and plans. So many plans. Both agreed they would have at least four children (probably more) because neither could fathom life for a child with fewer than three siblings. It would be cruel! The new house was designed with five bedrooms and a study that both secretly believed would become a necessary bedroom but didn't mention because they didn't want to scare the other.

The decisions about fittings and fixtures were agonised over, fought about and threatened to divide them until they both acknowledged that she was being uncharacteristically fierce. She was cranky and far more emotional than usual, her temper as likely to yield a flurry of tears as it was rage. And they realised; she was late. More than a month late, in fact, but the house and work had distracted them both. They were aflame with wonder and shame, knowing they should've been paying better attention, sobbing with joy and unable to stop touching each other. In a vacuum of love and reverence, he worshipped her body and whispered about her being a goddess, an angel, the mother of his child, life bearer and his life bringer. She glowed and floated somewhere above the world, imagining herself as he spoke of her, stunned and terrified.

They shouldn't have spoken of it, it was too early, really, but they were young and healthy and proud of their accomplishment. The mention of hoping the house was complete within nine months to one mother was enough to ignite the wildfire of the family party line and it took no time at all before *everyone* knew. Of course, they knew they shouldn't know, so clasping her hand, looking into her eyes and squealing became the first thing done at every family gathering, along with slapping him on the back. She was complimented and asked about timing, to which she demurred and admitted she hadn't been to a doctor yet. Her lower abdomen was cupped and giggles erupted as a tiny bump was described, even if nobody could see a thing.

It was just over two months before she finally got an appointment and by then, it was too late.

The doctor frowned at the blood test results, apparently immune to their joyful quivering as she was ushered onto an examination table for the ultrasound. Later, she would recall that she noticed everything in a very specific order: the gel was cold, the pressure on her full bladder was excruciating, the screen didn't show anything in a baby shape, the doctor's face was set in stone... the doctor's eyes were sad and worried. The doctor spoke slowly and gently, as if she were a child, not the one having one, and she was told that she was wrong. They'd both got it very, very wrong.

Numbness encapsulated them as the word

'tumour' was used instead of 'foetus' and 'aggressive action required' and 'hysterectomy' were spoken instead of 'birth plan'. She didn't understand how the thing inside her was a nightmare when everything else was a dream, how it was not a beginning at all, but an unequivocal ending. She looked to him, needing him to light her way out of the darkness but he was as bereft as she, an abyss of loss and confusion.

Life unfolded as it will inevitably do and they became lost in actions. Action was necessary and easier than thinking or feeling. The operation was inevitable and no amount of tears or regret could stop it. The house was finished and while she was curled in a ball staring at an anonymous hospital wall, he completed a final inspection and accepted the keys to a building that was merely a tomb for all their innocent dreams.

They tried. They moved into the sepulchre, filling its empty rooms with stuff, as if it could seal the gaping wounds in their souls. They accepted visitors and nodded at the outpourings of grief until they could take no more useless words and stopped people coming around. They slept beside each other in chemical-induced vacuity, miles and years and savage wedges of broken hearts apart. She did her best not to hate her own traitorous body and he did his best not to resent the changes in her but, in the end, they both failed. Neither could see their way past the expectations they'd constructed of Their Future, neither could forgive its death. She wasn't the hopeful, glimmering creature of myth she'd been and he couldn't bear her pain or resolve the new, black version of her with his love. He couldn't forgive her betrayal; she couldn't forgive his failure and, one day, they stopped. They stopped trying to resurrect the past and acknowledged the impossibility of their new normal. Lives and assets were divided, futures were laid to rest and blame was handed out like party favours.

In amongst this fury of reconciliation and regret, one victor stood tall. Silent, malevolent and triumphant, cancer saw without eyes the destruction it had caused, heard without ears the torment it had inflicted and savoured without lips the particular bitterness of the broken. And its purpose was fulfilled.

PICK A CARD, ANY CARD
A J R Fraser

It all started with the ace of hearts. A simple card, with a small capital 'A' printed in the corner and a large red heart emblazoned in the centre. You're thinking—the letter 'A', why it's just the first letter in the alphabet, and the heart is the symbol for love, so you probably could look at this as a story about first love. But as history has shown us—first love is often a tragic tale. Could it be therefore that the ace of hearts is a red card because red is the colour of blood? What does the 'Ace of Hearts' mean to you? Does it paint a picture of what we truly desire? What we truly want... or need... or love?

He placed the ace of hearts back into the deck, and then looked deeply into her almond eyes. His charming white smile and his beautiful baby blues caught her breath, as she uncomfortably hid behind a childish giggle.

How did you do that? Her eyes queried.

'It's a secret,' he winked. 'And you know what they say; a magician never tells. And if I tell you, I'd have to kill you.' To which he chuckled.

He lifted the glass of wine to his mouth, took a delicate sip and then he slowly licked the red from his wet lips as he admired his prey. She was not his type, too much perfume, too much makeup, too much sparkle. The image she portrayed was fake, the emotions she displayed were fake, and the life she was living was fake. As he looked around the tiny lounge room, he felt he was looking at another lie, a manufactured creation to this artificial existence. He needed to destroy this worthless relationship that was corrupting his fragile emotions. But he couldn't, because he was in love.

'Can I get you another glass of wine?' he asked her.

Her bewitching smile beckoned more than just wine, and it was that wicked painted face that quite often toyed with his weak emotions. He desperately needed another drink, so he hastily stepped into the kitchen.

He poured a glass of red wine, devoured it and then poured another. His emotions and thoughts were eroding his confidence and destroying his identity. He needed this relationship to end, as it was not good for him. She was a lie. She didn't complement him; she didn't encourage or add value to his life. It was time to cut her loose. Cut those emotional draining strings that kept pulling him back to her. Cut her out of his life... Cut... Cut...

Cut...

His nervous hand grasped the large kitchen knife, as he strode back into the lounge room. She smiled at him with sarcastic confidence, a belief that he didn't have the nerve to do anything. He felt those almond eyes mocking him. That vapid evilness from her soul was slowly smothering his existence, so he rushed forward and plunged the knife deep into her chest. She hissed at him, as that lifeless expression on her face didn't change. He thrust the knife deeper, she hissed again, but continued that cynical stare into his now corrupted soul.

A surge of erotic pleasure coursed through his body as he watched the knife pierce her. His breathing quickened as he pushed the knife harder and deeper. But that huge adrenalin rush of sensual excitement quickly evaporated, as grief and remorse took a firm grip of his heart.

What have I done? Oh no, she's dead. In total shock and disbelief he quickly reached for the phone and dialled the police.

'I've killed her,' he continuously screamed down the phone, in panic. 'I've killed her. I've killed her.'

Several minutes later with flashing lights and blaring sirens, there were a number policemen franticly bashing on the front door. As he opened it, several officers charged in with their pistols raised, screaming orders. They pinned him to the floor, his hands cuffed tightly behind his back.

'I'm sorry, I'm sorry.' He kept on yelling. 'I didn't mean to stab her. She just drives me crazy. I love her.' Tears flowed down his cheeks. 'I'm sorry, I'm sorry. I love her.'

A young officer gestured for the senior sergeant to enter the lounge room.

'What are we going to do about that, sir?' The officer pointed to the deflated Japanese sex doll, which lay sprawled across the lounge with a large kitchen knife protruding from its chest.

INSIDE THE BOX

Duncan Richardson

Janey

The wrapping was shiny and the scents that wafted out of that cardboard cavern were intoxicating. Inside was a black silk dress. I held it up. Howard had never bought clothes for me before.

'Where did you get this?' I gasped.

He laughed, hugging me. 'Oh Janey, just a special little retro place I've found.'

'But it's not my birthday.'

His eyebrows went up. 'So? Can't I spoil you?'

I couldn't quite believe we were talking like that. It was like the return of the old Howard; funny, romantic, surprising, before he was drowned by the drudgery of an office job.

When we were having dinner, my confusion grew when he said. 'You know, I quite like you not working.' As usual, I'd done the cooking. He noticed my wide eyes. 'Oh I don't mean you don't work at home, it's just that... You know. It's sort of comfortable. Like in the old days.'

So the next afternoon, there I was in the black silk dress with red stockings, sitting by the front door, doing the best Marilyn Monroe impression I could manage. And he loved it. Didn't notice my accent was way off. Within about five minutes we were making love on the floor like we'd just invented it, so even I started thinking maybe it was a great way to go.

I hadn't chosen to be out of work, it was just more State Government cuts, so I didn't really have a plan for my free days. It was good to be looked after for a change too, especially having been dumped by the Department. I felt like I was due for some TLC. And I thought of everyone at work, while I luxuriated in my silky lair.

Howard

I could say my old radios told me to do it. I could claim I was hearing voices. I didn't want to hurt Janey. Didn't even want to lock her up. But what else could I do?

'The music is OK,' she said. 'Maybe even the clothes every so often but not all the time. And only if we're going out somewhere nice. I don't want to live in the Fifties.'

But I do. I want a world where kids played outside most of the time and no one sat for hours in bloody internet cafes playing stupid games with someone they've never met and probably never will. I want a city where buildings were made to be looked at and lingered over.

'Look,' Janey said. 'People back then didn't think it was so wonderful. Look at the soppy way they went on about what a cynical age it was. You know, in that Christmas Special on your CD. 1952 for God's sake! They were moaning about kids who didn't believe in Santa Claus!'

'So what?' I said. 'I'm not looking for Utopia. And yeah, I know I can't have that world for real. But at least I can have a small part of it again. Here. Now.'

And when I turn on the old radios and they've warmed up and start humming, I can hear the old voices coming through. And then one of them whispered to me, '*Lock her up, in the spare room.*'

She yelled and screamed at me from behind the door. For over an hour. Lucky we're on a big block. Lucky we've got the river on one side and a park on another. Lucky I'd chosen a strong old-fashioned type of lock. She tried the windows but I'd already thought of that. Bolts inside and out. She called out, begging me to let her out, saying she didn't mean it, promising she wouldn't really leave me, she was just angry and wanted to give me a shock. But I'm not dumb enough to believe she wouldn't go. Not now. She'd be off like a rocket and then I'd be all alone in my time machine.

Give her a few days to let the idea sink in. Then she might see what I'm getting at. I've always loved the idea of time travel. I s'pose that's what I'm really hanging out for. But for now, I'll just turn the radio up a bit louder. Try to catch *The Lone Ranger* or whatever's floating by on the ether. See what the voices have to say.

Janey

He asked me a few weeks ago, would I like him to start using Brylcream. Jesus bloody Christ! What can you say to that? Anyway, he started using it. Just a bit at first, so people at work wouldn't notice but before too long they did notice. He told me, with that hang dog expression he gets. And at work it made him feel even more of an outsider. But he kept on singing under his breath, *'A little dab'lll do ya, the girls will all pursue ya.'*

'Honey, I'm home,' he called out one afternoon, about 2.30. There wasn't a shred of a joke in his voice.

I ran to the front door. 'What's happened?' I said.

He sighed. 'I've quit.' He dumped his bag on the floor. 'Slung me hook.' He started sobbing. I led him into the living room and sat him down on the sofa. 'I've had enough,' he said. 'I'm not going to be the butt of their jokes anymore.' He switched his eyes to me. 'Why aren't you wearing....?'

I stood up. 'Shit, if you expect me to prance around the place in silk gowns with the work I have to do around this creaky old house, you must be...'

He nodded slowing, gazing far off. 'That's what

they said. That's what did it. That's why I quit.' His eyes were green and watery. 'Maybe I am a weirdo like they say. Do you want me to become another soulless bastard ripping people off?' He buried his head in the cushions.

I could've laughed. The thought of Howard turning into some kind of pin-striped monster. I patted him off to sleep like a child. Tomorrow, I thought, something has to change.

So I laid my cards on the table, thinking I had a winning hand. Except he wasn't playing with the same deck. Apologised later, like he always does. Then he suggested I treat myself to a day out. With my sister or a friend, whoever.

Howard
Now Janey's yelling at me, 'You could get years for this!' Deprivation of liberty or something but I don't care. I'm already doing my time

My grandparents gaze at me from their photo on the piano, looking awkward, like they're weren't used to cameras. At first I thought they'd be angry with me for desecrating their old house. But now it's as if they understand.

It's quiet now. Janey must've fallen asleep. Half her luck. I've never been what you might call a good sleeper. I love these small hours. The present loses its grip and the past can slide back. So I put the radio on. There they are. The voices. Stan and Betty, my grandparents, not so much talking, more like a gentle humming. Saying, it's all right...

Janey

We were listening to the radio one morning. It was one of those 'classics' stations. There was a track by the Deltones from 1964. The DJ said, 'Ah they were more innocent times. There you were, just bopping along...'

Howard turned to me, looking pale against the pillow. 'He's right you know.'

I laughed. 'Maybe *we* were more innocent then because we were kids but the grownups were out there killing each other just like now.' I watched his face. No impact. I searched my memory for a war. 'Vietnam.'

I decided to do some research of my own. I went to the State Library and looked up the newspapers from the 1950s and 1960s.

That night, at dinner, I said, 'Howard, you know the whaling station opened on Moreton Island in the Fifties and the sand was red with blood? The cops searched out Bodgies to bash them. You could be arrested just for dancing in Brisbane back then. Howard just let his eyes drop to the floor and he turned away in one smooth movement.

Howard

It's how we lived in our hearts that was different. It's how we rested in our skins. The way people had patience and time to listen. The important thing was how the future looked when we dared to look at it.

I don't anymore. I can't.

Janey

When he locked me up, I raged then pleaded. I exhausted myself and flaked out on the bed.

When I opened my eyes it was early morning and a tray with breakfast on it was sitting there along with sandwiches wrapped in plastic. The bastard! Though it gave me an idea. Of course he doesn't want me to starve. So, sooner or later he would have to bring me more food.

Then an urging in my bowels gave me another idea. 'Howard,' I yelled. 'I need to go to the toilet.' That's got him. No ensuite in this place. I heard his aging slippers padding down the corridor, then his breathing on the other side of the door. 'Come on Howard, you're not going to make me pee my pants are you?' I was feeling better already. I heard him singing, *'When my sugar walks down the street, all the little birdies go tweet tweet tweet'.*

'Janey,' he said his voice slightly high. 'Janey, there's a chamber pot under the bed. You'll have to use that for now.' And he shuffled off.

God! I thumped on the door so loudly I almost did wet myself. But it was no good. In the end, I had to use his granny's old potty.

Howard

I hated making her do that but I needed time to work things out. And you know what women are like. Always needing to go to the toilet every five minutes.

Janey

I tried using the smelly potty as a blackmail tool but Howard just waited till I was asleep again and emptied it then. I knew he'd always beat me at staying awake. He found it hard enough to get his eyes to shut at the best of times.

It was weird, being a prisoner and waited on like a small child. Maybe if we'd had a kid, things would've been different. It's not so easy to live in the past when you've got a mouth to feed and a bum to wipe at regular intervals.

A line from one of Howard's old adventure shows kept driving me mad. *We always carry a few tools for emergencies such as these.* 'The Golden Boomerang'. But of course I didn't have any tools because being held prisoner was not exactly part of my normal life.

The moment came like this.

I was reaching up to the top of the wardrobe out of sheer boredom, to see what was there. Must've dislodged an old shoe box because next thing I know, it's sliding towards my face like a runaway train. 'Ouch,' I said quietly as it glanced by my cheek. That was it. Like the staged fight in all the old prison escape movies. The staged accident.

I looked around the room. A few books on a shelf. Some photos, a small mirror and a comb on the dresser. An old green suitcase up high on the wardrobe... That would do. I crept to the door and listened. No radio. Nothing. Back to the wardrobe and pulled the case. It hit the ground with a thud. I cried out. 'Argh! Help!'

Nothing.

I crept back to the door. No sound. Bastard's gone out, I thought. So I waited.

Finally, around eight that night, I heard Howard in the lounge room. I looked around frantically for something heavier to add to the case. My toe kicked it. The potty. Empty, luckily. I stuffed it into the case, added the books for extra bulk and hauled the case back on top of the cupboard.

I'd have to make it really hit me. My acting wasn't good enough, to bung it on. I readied myself for the pain, then pulled the case.

Crash! It landed on my foot and shook the floorboards. I screamed, letting all my rage at Howard flood out, while trying not to laugh. I hobbled over behind the door, ready, hoping the bloody potty hadn't wrecked my chances by breaking a toe,

'Janey?' he called. 'Are you okay?'

I kept on sobbing as best I could. Howard was now mumbling outside the door. Keys rattled.

A cold shock ran through me. What could I do to stop him just blocking the door? He was bigger than me after all.

The case lay on the floor. I grabbed it. The door opened slowly. I hoisted the case over the door and heard a thud. 'Ooff!' A stumble. Another thud. Limbs collapsing.

I peered round the door. Howard was out cold. I felt his pulse. Still going. Must've hit his head on the dresser. His face was shockingly grey. Shit. 'You stupid bastard, Howard,' I hissed. 'Now look what you've made me do.'

Howard

hi my names Howard and iv got to rite sumfing evry day my doctor says it will help my memry but I fink my memrys reelly good alredy

my girl frend jany tells me that it is wen she comes to see me speshully wen she plays sum music and we dans dont no why but jany offen cries then so I tell her a joke and it helps a bit

Janey

I can't stay away of course though it tears my guts out when I see the way he is. Everyone's been very good, sympathizing about 'the accident' and offering help endlessly. The tyranny of help, disguising the assumption that sooner or later I'm going to take Howard home and look after him. Money's no object his parents say.

At least he'd be happy he's in the Royal Brisbane. The old part. Though none of that seems to matter to him anymore.

When we dance and he moves like a man, a young man with music in his blood, I sometimes whisper things to him, hoping that somehow the old saner Howard is still in there and will come rushing out. But yesterday I couldn't take it anymore and started muttering 'You've really trapped me this time, you bastard' and I couldn't help myself, I kicked him in the shins.

Should've seen the hurt on his face.

So easy to hurt you, Howard, I thought. That's always been your trouble. Born in the wrong time.

Howard

sumtimes wen we dans I can sort of hear another voys in my ears an I feel reel grown up but wen the musics stopt I cant remember it anymore wun time janey sed well youve sort of got your wish havent you but I dont no wot shes torking about

come on janey I sed sing it with me wun mor time

im holdin you in my holden...

Acknowledgement to the poem 'Hint, Hint' by Robert Morris in his book 'Thangool Road' for the inspiration.

GALLERY, 1
EJA

She worked at the zoo for three years and never got tired of doing tours. The kids with their little attention spans. The teens who pretended not to like animals, but who still made sure to see their favourites. The adults who didn't even try to hide their awe. Yes, she thought, this was her dream job.

FIFTEEN TO THE TOP

Margaret Dakin

Last night I was looking forward to seeing her as I mounted the stairs—fifteen of them, all the way to the top. I get from her what I don't get at home.

I opened the door and she was there—naked, sitting on the mattress, her back against the wall, legs drawn up under her. She was dishevelled, but in the faint moonlight that comes in through the window and washes her body, nothing could spoil her beauty. She looked so young; not much older than my daughter would have been.

As I had expected she was a lot calmer. When I gave her the carton of food, she snatched it and wolfed it down, then took a swig of water from the bottle I handed her, all the while keeping her eyes on me. Who could believe she would be so easy to please?

The first couple of nights she was not so placid.

She threw the take-away cartons across the room where they still lie. She was shivering and rubbing her arms. 'Don't want food. Haven't you got anything for me,' she screamed, 'not even a joint? I need something.'

I shook my head. 'It's for your own good.' I threw her the blanket.

But the next night when I came the mattress was wet with her perspiration and other bodily fluids. The empty water bottle was pressed to her cracked lips. She was babbling on—something about, 'Jack, Jack, stay where you are. Wait for me there. I won't be long.'

I rocked her in my arms and let a trickle of water run into her mouth. She opened her eyes. They seemed to have sunk so far back into their sockets that, in the dim light, I thought I was holding a skeleton – my nightmare become real. 'Sorry Jenny, I'm so sorry,' I said.

She shook her head. 'I'm not your Jenny.'

'You need to give up the heroin. It'll kill you.' I crooned as we swayed back and forth.

'Yeah, I will, I promise,' she whispered. 'I'll do anything you want if you just let me go.'

I've seen them all—addicts, and young kids just out for an innocent night of partying. They all look the same when they're dead; like it was all just a mistake.

It was raining when I picked her up in the Valley

where she was working her usual patch. She was trying to keep dry, as they all were, none of them standing on the edge of the road showing a leg or mouthing obscenities at the passing cars.

She didn't usually do that anyway. I'd watched her for a while and figured she only worked for as long as it took to fund a supply of coke or smack, and then she would disappear for a few days. She didn't seem to really want to be there. That's why I chose her.

I went over to where she stood in the doorway of the dark shop. I could feel the rain soaking the floppy brim of my cloth hat, drops hesitating for a moment on the end of my nose then falling to catch on my belly. Knew I looked pathetic. Could hardly see her, my glasses were so fogged up. I took them off and wiped them on my shirt. Only made things worse.

I asked her how much; she told me and I jerked my head in the direction of my ute on the other side of the road. She slipped off her high heels and we ran across. She had on a leather jacket and she hunkered into it as she danced from one foot to the other waiting for me to unlock the door. She slid in and I saw her legs under the short skirt were white with the cold. As she flicked the tangled wet hair from her neck I tossed her an old blanket that was on the driver's seat.

'Mind if we go for a ride?' I said.

'Time's money. You paying extra?'

'Don't expect you to do it for love.'

Took her to a bit of bush I know out Redbank Plains way. We parked on the bank of a shallow creek. The rain had stopped and the full moon had come out from behind the clouds, so bright the trees had shadows. We could hear the water running over rocks.

I opened the door to let her out and again she was jittery, stamping her feet. 'Be a nice place for a picnic,' she said. 'My mum used to bring me to a place like this when she was

working in the hotel. Wish we hadn't moved from that town. One of the teachers at the school was real nice and I made a friend. Alice her name was.'

She looked at me and smiled and I reached over and lifted a strand of her long fair hair. It was dry now, and soft. I wanted to comfort her and look after her. She was just a lonely kid. She's worth saving, I thought.

'Do you like picnics?' I said. 'I used to bring my daughter here for a picnic. Know what it's called? Happy Jack Gully.' I grinned.

Her laugh was full of bitterness Then I saw her eyes glisten and tears formed in the corners, spilling over and running down beside her nose.

'My son was called Jack,' she said. 'He would have liked this place.'

'Where is he now?'

'He got killed—run over by a truck. I keep seeing his face – smiling, till he looked up and saw the truck—then kinda surprised. Too good for this world he was.' She rubbed her cheek with the back of her hand and licked the tears from her lips, scratching at her arms.

I reached out to touch her shoulder but she shook herself and pulled away, real jumpy.

'Never mind. I was a mess for a while there, wondering if I hadn't shouted he might just have made it – but I'm okay now.'

'I lost my daughter too,' I said. 'Not like you, in an instant, but gradually. You never get over it.'

She turned her head quickly and looked at me. 'No, you don't. But what about tonight? Want to do it here?'

I got to my feet thinking maybe I'd take her back to town, but decided she needed my help. 'Here's okay. Best get in the back of the ute. Ground's a bit damp.' I unfolded the tarp then tossed down the blanket.

We went through the motions of oral sex, but that was not what I wanted. 'Mind if I tie you up a bit?' I said.

She shrugged, 'Whatever turns you on, but I need to get back to town soon.'

I tied the rope around her waist, then wound it about her arms and upper body, and finally round one ankle and then the other.

She looked puzzled, then she stared at me with frightened eyes. 'What do you think you're doin'? Let go of me you pervert. Let me...'

She was struggling and I clamped my hand over her mouth. I pulled the gag from my pocket, stuffed it in her mouth and tied it at the back of her head, then fastened the blindfold over her eyes. I was thankful I'd got her tied up before she made too much of a fuss. Didn't want to use violence on her like I'd had to with the others. She was trying to scream as I threw the edge of the tarp over her and jumped out of the tray.

We drove to this old two-storey place. Used to belong to Mum and Dad. It's isolated and pretty well derelict. I wrapped her in the blanket and carried her up to the top floor, fifteen steps. I unwound the rope from her arms and legs and tied her to the hook screwed into a beam on the ceiling.

She tore off the blindfold, pulled the gag from her mouth. 'What are you gonna do to me?' she screamed. 'What is this place? Let me go.' She was crying at last.

This evening the bucket was a stinking mess. Must have been a couple of nights since I'd emptied it. How long had she been here? I counted the take-away containers—four on the floor and the fifth in my hand, still warm. I passed it to her and settled down beside her on the mattress. As she ate I stroked her leg and talked. She always listens without saying anything—a captive audience; but then I have got her tethered. The rope is around her waist but the knot is well out of her reach. I'm good at knots, all part of the training. She can only move away from the mattress as far as the bucket.

I tell her about the sights I've seen when I was driving the ambulance. No one else wants to hear. My wife never did. She hardly speaks to me these days. Blames me for what happened—eases her own guilt. Suppose she's right. Should have looked closer at what was happening in my own home. Too overwhelmed with the day-to-day horror of my life.

'You can't imagine what it's like to see somebody, still strapped in her seat, but her head's missing,' I tell the girl. 'In the back the kids are like rag dolls. Can't get it out of my brain, and when I shut my eyes I'm there again. Can't sleep, can't stay awake. Can you understand? You must understand.'

She just stares at me with frightened eyes.

'One young girl, worked on her for an hour, at the scene and on the way to the hospital. Her leg was almost severed, but she had internal injuries also. At first she screamed for me to help her, but then in the end she just looked at me as if all she wanted was for the pain to stop. Had to let her go; all so futile. Put out of my mind that those bodies were human beings. That's what we did. We pretended it was just a job, even made ghoulish jokes about it.'

Tonight I climb the stairs again. I've decided I'm going to finish it. She's resigned to whatever happens but when I left her last night she was like a caged animal—getting worse again, not better—scratching at her arms and screaming. She doesn't look like my daughter anymore. I thought I could prevent her from sharing Jenny's fate but now I see I'm powerless. I couldn't keep my own daughter away from drugs. I was a paramedic for christsake. Should've seen the signs as she progressed from party pills to the hard stuff. I was blind to where she was half the night. Out earning the money for the drugs—that's where.

I finally caught on when she started to look sick—my beautiful Jenny—like a skeleton with skin stretched over the bones—sores on her lips, coughing, crying, appealing to me out of huge eyes. 'Help me, Dad. I don't want to die.'

I cradled her in my arms like a baby. 'We'll book you into a clinic. You'll be right soon.' But she only lasted a few days before she signed herself out.

When we found her it was too late. We put her to bed and now I was the one with the syringe, trying to keep her pain at bay. In the end, like the girl in the accident, she just wanted it to finish. She was almost peaceful. I was the one raging against fate. 'Jenny baby, hold on. We can do it.' But all I could do was watch it happening. I stroked her limp hair and cursed God.

The girl I've got tethered on the end of the rope, she was just like Jenny—at first full of fear, then angry, then resigned. At times she was hopeful. 'If I give you what you want will you let me out of here?

I'll meet you every week—two, three times a week—we could have such good times. You can do what you want to me—tie me up, anything. For you it would all be free.'

Sometimes she'd cry. 'Please, please, please. I never hurt you.'

Now I think she's given up everything, even thinking. She knows I'm going to have to kill her, like the others.

How many have I killed? Two with the knife but they turned out to be real sluts—foul-mouthed, malignant, evil inside and out. But how many others have I failed to save that I might have if I'd done something differently. A waste of space.

Fifteen to the top—I'm here. I push the door open so hard it slams back against the wall. I have the knife in my hand. She starts to shake her head. Her eyes are big like Jenny's, looking at me, pleading. She doesn't cry out or try to get away.

I pick up the bucket and overturn it. The contents spread slowly across the floor like a plague. Then I slash at my wrists with the knife—but that'd take too long.

I pull down the loose end of the rope and make a loop, tie one of my special knots—a hangman's noose. Then I put it over my head, the knot under my ear, and stand on the bucket.

The last thing I see as I kick the bucket away is the girl—staring at me with terrified eyes, backing away as far as she can. Briefly it crosses my mind that, considering the state she is in, she won't last long with no one to provide take-away.

But she doesn't really want to live anyway.

GRASS GREEN

JH Nelson

Standing amidst the rows of clothes in our wardrobe, I unzip and shimmy out of my dress. Steve finally took me out to *Sequins* for dinner tonight. It was alright—of course, it would have been better if he'd taken me three months ago when it was new. Now the suggestively titled *The Italian Touch* has opened and is getting amazing reviews. It's bringing in big names, or so I've heard.

'Need some help, gorgeous? Always happy to help you and your cute toosh undress.' Steve grins provocatively at me.

'Not tonight. I've got a headache from the wine.'

'Oh Beccy, you barely had two glasses.' He walks away, pulling his shirt tails out. I climb into bed alone.

Up early for work, the tubes and containers of products that litter the vanity would put a beauty parlour to shame. They are all part of my strict daily regimen. Giving each of them time to work their magic, I apply foams, creams and oily serums to my hair, face and body. They're all designed to keep me at my peak. A final glance at the mirror; I have outdone myself. My hair and makeup look great against the new dress. The royal blue makes my eyes pop. When I saw it on sale, I just had to have it. Shutting off the lights, I can leave the penthouse apartment knowing I've done my best.

Work is hectic. My boss Josh has several deals being finalised this week which adds to my usual load. My smile is firmly in place. Mum's words are ingrained in me, 'Always remember the swan, Rebecca, gliding gracefully across the lake. No one wants to see the work going on below the surface now, do they?'

Too busy to notice the time, I haven't heard the arrival of Josh's wife Sandra until they stand together at my desk.

'I'm taking Sandra out for lunch today, Rebecca. Please take messages while I'm gone, and I'll deal with them when I get back.'

'Sure. I'm almost finished with these contracts. I'll put them on your desk for your perusal when they're done, shall I?'

'Excellent. Thanks.'

Watching them leave hand in hand I could almost snarl. Sandra is wearing the new shoes I was drooling over yesterday. I call Steve. It goes to voicemail, so I leave a message telling him I will be home late tonight because of all the contracts I have to organise. It is a half-truth. I do have a lot of deals and paperwork to get through, and I will be home late. If I leave the bags in the car until he's asleep, he won't even notice them in the wardrobe tomorrow.

I'm still seething over the shoes when Josh and Sandra return. I all but froth at the mouth when I find out that he took Sandra to *The Italian Touch*. What does a girl have to do? What does Sandra have? Well, besides the damn shoes I want! Taking a punt, I see if I can't make her squirm, just a little.

'I love your shoes, Sandra. They're from the new 'Lussuria' designer range, aren't they?' I challenge.

'Oh, thank you, yes they are. I felt so spoilt when Josh surprised me with them two nights ago.'

I blanch hearing that Josh bought them for her. I guess I shouldn't be surprised. I smile meekly and make my excuses to get back to work, a new round of fury building in my stomach. After they wander away from my desk, I open a new internet tab. At the click of a button, I rearrange funds from one account to the next. Their final destination is my credit card—wow, it has never looked so healthy. Too bad it will be gone by tonight. But oh, the beautiful shoes I will have. Absolutely worth it!

Feeling refreshed and excited to show off my new purchases tomorrow at the office, I carefully tuck the bags into the rear foot well of the car. I drape a black bath towel over them. They become invisible in the dim lighting of the undercover carpark. A trick I've used many a time before.

Empty-handed except for my handbag, I enter the apartment to discover Steve playing video games on the console he insisted on having. My eyes roll so far around that I think I actually strain one. Can that actually happen? I ignore him and move to the ensuite where I can work on a sexy eye-shadow combination that will match my new dress. It'll be a challenge as I remember the dress. It has a unique shade, somewhere between emerald and lime. It's grass green if I think about it. With new shoes to match, I play around with some bronze tones. It isn't long before Steve finds me.

'Hey Bec, I was doing some banking this afternoon, and there's twelve hundred missing from our first account. You know anything about that?' His eyebrows are raised.

'I told you I was going to pay those few bills we had on the fridge. I didn't add them up, but...' I shrug, trailing off.

'But you didn't pay them. I know that because I just checked them. That's why I was *doing* the banking!'

'Oh, sorry. I was online today at work, maybe I pressed something accidentally. I'm sure I've just moved it into the wrong account, or something. I'll fix it, don't worry, babe.'

'Don't lie, Rebecca! You took money out of our account and put it on your credit card. Except now your credit card is maxed out again. What did you buy this time? Huh? More clothes, shoes, make-up, hats, what? And don't you *dare* lie to me!' Steve is in a rage. My chin quivers and I whimper. Tears build and fall from my lids.

'This isn't my fault. If you earnt more, we wouldn't have this problem!'

He gasps an ugly laugh. 'For every dollar I make, you spend ten! I could never earn enough money to satisfy you. Not even your precious Josh earns that much!'

I slam the bathroom door in Steve's face and push the latch down so he can't get in. Tears fall faster now and leave muddy tracks down my cheeks as they collect everything from foundation to eye-liner and mascara in their path.

If only I had a man like Josh.

BLACK SPOT

Peta Fitzpatrick

Tuesday: mid-morning, mid-term, 1983

Sister Mary Xavier is drunk – solid, heavy, staying-put drunk. This in itself is not unusual. Same drunk nun slouched in same vinyl armchair. But today is different. Today she isn't snorting her way in and out of consciousness, muttering her usual 'helpful suggestions'...'tip of the tongue behind the teeth, girl', 'project, project, don't yell it child!'

Today she sleeps. Her undulating snore the backdrop to our speech and drama lesson.

Stout, sweet Miss, *never Miz*, O' Flannery, with her healthy moustache and her endearingly ugly beret takes us through exercise after exercise, preparing us for yet another round of exams. As we slide through our circumflex inflections and practise our alveolar stops, the bobble on top of her beret wobbles double-time against Xavier's snores.

At lesson's end, the room empties save for me – and the still sleeping nun. As the last out, it's my job to close the windows. As I near Xavier's chair and reach to drag the window shut, her hand grabs my wrist and pulls me down towards her. Bleary eyes wide – looking straight into mine. 'It's a lie! It's always been a lie! Don't let them...' Then sleep sends her back into her usual slump.

Tuesday: late in the afternoon
I know I'm being watched. I've been watched constantly this afternoon. Why they would bother, I don't know. I'm sure bringing in the washing for Nan can't be that exciting. But there are eyes on me. I feel them as keenly as I did Sister Xavier's fingers on my arm. Whoever they are, they've always been watching me.

Did *they* see her talking to me? Not that it could matter, surely – the ramblings of an old lush. She's sat in that armchair for years, sloshed and harmless, while countless girls stood before her and learned to enunciate in the capable hands of Miss O. It *was* weird, but not worth dwelling on. So why are they watching me so intently?

Tuesday: deep in the night
My heart's pounding. Even now I'm under their scrutiny – I can feel it on my skin. I just need to sleep! 'Sod off!' I hiss through gritted teeth...

...and wake hours later with a pounding

headache.

Wednesday: after morning maths' class

One of the factory model sports teachers asks me to deliver a set of keys to the Ignatius building before chapel. *Whatever you want Miss...just call me servant!* My head still throbs, an insistent beat that matches my footsteps. On my way back from Ignatius, I take a shortcut behind the convent and see Sr Xavier shambling along the verandah towards the dining room. She calls me over, 'Girl! Girl!' I shake my aching head, (*oww!*) 'I'm late for chapel Sister!' I call, hurrying past, not relishing the thought of an errand that may well end in my getting caught with a scotch bottle. As I whip past her, I hear again 'It's a lie...'

Moments later, I'm sitting in a crowded pew in the hot chapel, watching the sun pour through the stained glass, turning Maeve's limp hair green (with envy?) and Snobby Sarah's mane blood red. I let out a half giggle at the thought of the word 'stained', imagining that blood red...blood...red... against Sarah's tanned neck, coursing down her shoulders...

The mass lasts forever. Father Joseph drones on. I notice only colours, and hear a strange faint hiss over the odd word from the priest—'sacrifice', 'faithful', 'miracle', 'transubstantiation'. And now another voice, close to my ear – vitriolic, spitting 'Shut up. Shut up Xavier, you old drunk!' My eyes dart around cautiously, seeing no-one but bored schoolgirls, fed-up teachers, and nuns, ever vigilant for minor infractions. And then the voice changes, is closer, inside me, wrapped around my spine, filling my whole body with 'You know it is *not* a lie, girlie! The drunk knows nothing...'

Wednesday afternoon: nearly bell-time

Normally, I love Ancient History, my favourite class. Today, I don't want to think about Egyptian mummification processes, about removing organs in gruesome and inventive ways. My headache is back with a vengeance, my ears feel blocked. I don't want to imagine the warm, wet slide of the discrete spoils of death against my skin as I work. To marvel at the careful preservation of each fragment of what was before a living thing, now a collection of precious parts. To hold the tools that make history. I don't want to listen to the voice that tells me of this noble work... and of the truth I'm yet to face... and of my purpose...

I only want to sleep.

Wednesday afternoon: the bus ride home

It's hot and my head is now filled with a constant fizz of static I have to fight through to hear properly. The boys from St Martin's stand over their bags, holding poles and straps. Their sweat wafts towards me in stale waves as warm air pushes through barely open windows. Mark and Jason are murmuring, heads close together, snickering. Jason looks over at me, raises an eyebrow in disdain and turns back to Mark, saying something that sets him off laughing. They both turn towards me, laughing harder, Mark slapping Jason on the arm in his mirth. Mortified, I squeeze my eyes shut...and all is frozen. I open them. Both boys are slumped on the bus floor... blood covering their still bodies, and I am alone. I clamp my hands over my eyes, the hiss in my head is unbearable. I blink twice, raise my head and once more, both boys stand before me. I hear something about rowing and that morning's training session, a continued conversation... I...I don't think they've even given me a thought.

Yet I can't help remembering the instant of warm satisfaction at seeing them stained red, like Sarah's shoulders in the chapel this morning.

Wednesday night: just before midnight

I can't get comfortable. The pain and the hiss in my head have faded but my limbs feel twitchy. I can hear something. A quiet, tinny voice... like a radio in the next room. I drift off. Then awake with a start as in my left ear, clear as day, I hear 'Have you remembered yet? Have you figured it out? What Xavier was lying to you about?' I shake my head to quiet the voice. 'No? I see. Not as clever as I'd hoped'. I stammer 'Rem..embered what? Figured what out?'

'The big truth... remember The Big Truth? ... It made you who you are... who you are becoming. Remember good, pious Sister Theresa telling you all about your soul? You were six, or was it seven? That soul that should have been white when you came into this world? So sad...so sad... Born with a black stain on your soul, a black mark, a black spot... and nothing, nothing to make it go away'. The voice twisted around to my other ear, crooning 'Everything you do wrong only makes it worse. You can't wish it away, can't wash it away, not you, only him, only when you die. Remember making up some nasty little girl sins to confess to Father Mark? So he'd believe you? Believe what a bad girl you were? You know it's a sin to lie to a priest, don't you? Yesss... that Black Spot's just got bigger and bigger... That's why they watch you, you know! Everyone up there watches you, plus their host of holy spies, here on earth. They all know what you're thinking. And they're bad thoughts, aren't they?'

I feel something strange on my face. My fingers come away wet. In the darkness I know that what I can feel are the tears of inevitability. And the noise in my head is back tenfold.

Thursday: just before last lesson
I have spoken to no one for days, other than out of necessity. I think the bus driver is the one who has heard the most from me since Tuesday. A Tuesday that feels like a lifetime ago. I'm becoming used to the Poltergeisty-End-of-Transmission-hiss filling my head. Going through the motions of lessons, eating, walking from building to building for each

class, it hits me that a strange new sense of purpose is keeping me moving. It's not...quite...clear, but there is something I have to do to make this hissing stop. If I can find just one quiet moment, I will know...and this will be over.

I need a signal. A sign. That's what the saints prayed for, so, why not? If it worked for them, why is it such a strange thing for me to look for? The hiss! .... I cover my ears, no use. Instead of heading upstairs to Italian, I duck into the curved grotto, the tall hedging hiding me once I am inside. Dumping my bag on the grass, I stand before the cracked white statue of Mary with her hands out and eyes cast downwards. She is missing a little finger. Positioning myself underneath her, I sit, her gaze falling directly on me. 'Ok. Do it! Give me something' I plead with her, never taking my eyes off hers. Nothing. The hiss and I wait together... An ant crawls down her face, across one of her blank eyes. My head is pure static now. I can't even think, can only watch the ant, black against her white neck, across her shoulder, down her arm, down. The Hiss is unbearable, my eyes go in and out of focus. The ant reaches the end of Mary's sleeve, then, across the back of her hand, into a crack left by the missing finger and is gone.

A light shines directly into my eyes through the hedge leaves. I look up squinting. The static in my head has tuned itself to my heart's rhythm, and is beating with urgency. The light, the sun's reflection, off an old, uneven windowpane set in stone walls behind the grotto. Is this my sign? 'Yesss'…answers the Hiss. I pick up my bag, full of tools that make history, make herstory. A black stain on my soul, a black mark, a black spot. The sun is catching the drama room windows.

Thursday: fifteen minutes to last bell
Sister Mary Xavier, as one with her sagging chair, murmurs fitfully in her dreams. She lifts a hand and drops it in her lap, her slack cheeks quivering as she turns her head. I stand and watch her sleep… if it still is sleep after so much scotch. I look at the hand in her lap, at rest. The hissing turns things down a notch and a sense of calm rises. I can still hear her urgent 'It's a lie! It's always been a lie!' The ghost of a voice drifts up and out of me, growing from a murmur to a near shout, 'Shut up. Shut up Xavier, you old drunk!'

Her eyes snap open. The hissing stops. I smile.

In my hand is a Stanley knife, picked up in the art room hours before. It quivers with anticipation. *The tools that make history.* Across my vision crawls a black ant, disappearing into a crack where a finger should have been. Xavier raises her hands, conveniently, in defence. Her face a mask of fear, yet somehow comical. As I grab her hand I see the moment when she realizes my intention. I find her gurgling half-scream annoying at best, as removing a finger is a little more work than I'd anticipated. I snarl at her as I work 'Shut up you drunken fool. You know it's the truth. *You* are the liar. Black

Stain. Black Mark. Black Spot. Never come out. Nothing you can....oh!' and the finger is free. I put it in my pocket – the first in my collection of precious parts. She seems stunned, or maybe... yes, passed out. I appreciate the bliss of silence as I kneel and wipe my bloodied hand on her faded navy habit.

Silence from her. Silence in my head.

I sit back and lean against her stockinged legs. Warmed by the sun through the glass, I close my eyes, for just a little. So thankful for the sign in the grotto. For the peace in my head.

Then, a small shove. 'What are you doing girl, get up, get up!' Xavier is pushing at my shoulder. I turn, looking for the blood, confused at its absence. She pushes me again then recognizes me 'Oh, it's you. Come to listen to me now? Ready to listen to an old soak?'

Unable to speak, I nod, half risen, hands shaking, and fall into the seat beside her. My head still quiet, she begins...

'I see it in you girl. What the lie has done to you. You've shriveled up before you've lived. The fear has made you senseless. You bought every cruel word of it, didn't you? Without even realizing! The black stain. The black spot. It's all a lie. Have you never wondered? Wondered why they told babies they were bad? Nothing chases away strength like fear - deep, mortal, in-your-bones fear. Nothing stops you having opinions like judgement. Nothing makes you behave like being watched. Some resist it, resist the lie, some ...can't.' She points at her chest to make this point. 'Some...can't. Never wondered why I need my little tipples? It's a lie. It's always been a lie'.

I close my eyes, inhale. Exhale. Beside me, Sister Mary Xavier's quiet snores make me smile. I stand then, and look on her a while, wondering if her revelation is a step towards a strange kind of sainthood. The last bell of the day rings. I leave the room, schoolbag in one hand, a half-bottle of scotch dangling from the other.

DISCOVERING MR DENDY
Alicia Bruzzone

'It'll be different this time. You'll see.'

Minty watched through the jungle of overgrown grass as Mr Dendy kissed his wife fondly on the forehead before turning the key in their new home. There was hope on her careworn face. Minty had a huge painted smile on his face as two boys followed them into the awaiting house.

Most of the street observed the moving van back up the driveway, diesel fumes pluming over the agapanthus before the air brakes squealed through the quiet neighbourhood. Sweat was already beading off the two men who emerged from the cab. Over the course of the day their sweat increased to coursing streams as the truck slowly emptied. An entire life, boxed and hidden from sight.

Minty learnt that was exactly as they liked it.

The Dendys kept to themselves. Mrs Dendy worked while the two boys were at school, and Mr Dendy set to make the yard more hospitable. Minty had been spotted then. Mr Dendy had given him an odd look, but turned his back and went about his ways.

All autumn they appeared to be the average family. In summer, along with the parched earth, things began to crack.

It wasn't just Minty spying from the garden who could hear the arguments, the slammed doors. Eyes peeked through blinds up and down the road, and letter boxes were inspected more thoroughly than usual. When Mrs Dendy left for work in the morning she was thinner than she had been in all of the months they'd lived here, stressed as she buckled the two boys into the car. 'He's fighting a disease,' she'd explain in a gentle voice. 'He doesn't mean the things he says, it's just the demons inside trying to fight their way out. But your dad's strong, he'll beat them.'

She'd chew her nails nervously as she darted her eyes back to the closed curtains of the living room, eyes welling as if she was never sure what she'd find when she returned.

When Mr Dendy slunk out of the house and into a taxi, Minty watched on, wide eyed. He stared with a vacant expression when Mr Dendy reappeared an hour later, toting several heavy brown paper bags. They clinked together as he climbed the porch.

The house was silent and still until Mrs Dendy returned, somehow sensing something was up as she left the boys safely buckled in the car. Minty watched the entire event unfold.

'I think we might be out of milk,' Mrs Dendy told the children brightly, strain of the fake smile cracking her lipstick. 'I'll just run in and check.'

The youngest boy whimpered and cowered into his seat, while his stepbrother merely pressed his face to the glass in resigned defeat. This was not their first grocery run.

Mr Dendy was not dishevelled when Mrs Dendy opened the front door. He greeted his wife gaily, his affection doted in open kisses on her mouth.

'You're been drinking,' Mrs Dendy accused, wiping the taste of stale beer from her lips. 'You promised me! You said your choice was us!'

'Calm down, love,' Mr Dendy soothed, rubbing her arms with his palms. 'It was a hot one, and I was dying for a beer. It was just a beer, no harm done.'

Mrs Dendy nodded, and walked back to the car. Minty caught her talking to herself, assurances that it truly was just a beer, and she had nothing to worry about. She was causing problems again, wasn't he saying this was how she always caused problems? But she couldn't talk to him now about it when he was in such a good mood, she'd have to wait until tomorrow.

Minty saw nothing different in the morning routine as Mrs Dendy ferried the children to school on her way to work. Mr Dendy was louder today, but nothing obscene. Barely anybody bothered to peer out their curtains.

A week later and the fights were back. Mrs Dendy called in sick for work, her eye black as she hurried the children to the car. She'd tried to conceal the bruise under makeup and new bangs, but Minty was low in the grass, he saw the colours change throughout the week, the blues and purples melding to yellows and browns.

The recycling bin was full after Mrs Dendy tipped out the contents of the brown bags on the lawn, making quite the buzz over neighbouring fences.

Mr Dendy took the car this time. Minty had exhaust blown into his face as it shot backwards down the drive before roaring off. Mrs Dendy had chased him onto the porch, and now crumpled on the concrete as she sobbed at the retreating lights. What was she to do? He promised, he loved her. How could he do this?

The police were called the next time a scream was heard from the Dendy household. Minty watched as Mrs Dendy shook, but refused to talk to police. She was fine, just seen a mouse. No need for alarm. The boys were physically unscathed, and so they left.

Mr Dendy apologized on the porch, right there in front of Minty. He was so sorry, and he'd never do it again. He didn't know what he was thinking. His eyes glistened as he apologized for hurting her, like they would so many times as Minty watched on. Mrs Dendy stayed.

All through winter she stayed, as the grass grew longer and the boys took to climbing trees so they didn't have to go inside. Sometimes they'd play with Minty, more often than not his presence was simply ignored.

Minty heard the same excuses enough to memorize them. It was always an accident; Mr Dendy was always sorry. And he loved them, didn't they know that?

Mrs Dendy skipped too many days at work and was let go. She stayed home with Mr Dendy then, her once slender frame now emancipated as she tried to help her husband fight his demons. Most days he lost, but on the days he didn't the house would ring with laughter as everything was made right again, the cuts healed over as bruises were soothed. Minty watched those days, looked through the front window when the curtains were thrown back and a steady breeze was allowed to enter. Those were the days the neighbours didn't watch. Just Minty. Minty and an enormous smile.

Minty was the only one watching when the eldest boy was sent home from school early. From the heated argument that followed, the next few houses learned alongside Minty that he'd been suspended. Mrs Dendy wanted to solely deal with the fitting punishment, but Mr Dendy wouldn't have a bar of it. She was only his stepmother; she wouldn't know what to do.

Minty had already seen that today Mr Dendy let his demons win.

One blow was all it took for Mrs Dendy to finally resolve her niggling doubts. One strike to the boy and she decided. She would leave.

She tried to then, Minty heard her crushing sobs as Mr Dendy held her captive until her resolve broke. Then he sobered up, apologized, and promised it would never happen again.

The boys' backpacks bulged as they left for school the next morning. Atypically, Mr Dendy came to see them off. When underwear fell from the younger one's unzipped pocket, Mr Dendy thundered his wrath in the driveway. Neighbours snuck looks through cracks in curtains, while others phoned for support. Minty just watched, wide eyed, in his front row seat by the driveway.

He was there when Mrs Dendy said she was leaving for good, watching when she fought to get the boys free and locked in the car. He heard her find a courageous voice and tell Mr Dendy they had witnesses. Looked on as she started the car and left for the very last time. He was also closest when Mr Dendy gave into his consuming rage, and reached for a projectile.

Minty fell through the air, soaring into the reversing windscreen. His cheery red hat snapped first, little gnome legs crumbling on impact. Minty the garden gnome's wide eyes watched as Mrs Dendy wiped tears from her eyes with a steely glaze and sped faster, windscreen wipers frantically twitching past broken glass and concrete.

Minty's face rolled onto the tar of the road as police began to assemble, crushed in heavy footfall as Mr Dendy frantically dashed after his wife.

GALLERY, 2

EJA

We flick on the news and the headlines read; mass killing, theft, corrupt government. Our games filled with blood. The gap of poverty ever widening, ever growing. Spoken words, books and films showing ideas of a dimming society.

YELLOW SCARF

Lara Tomlinson

Allie entered my life the same way she left it, abruptly and mysteriously. The first time we locked eyes was unexpected but memorable. Her soulful eyes and genuine smile made her happiness contagious. She was like a colourful songbird, one of a kind and radiating life.

I felt something ignite as soon as our eyes met. From then on, her intrigue only grew.

No one knew why she had moved to our school, where she had moved from, or anything about her family. It was quite impressive for a high schooler's private life to remain unknown in a small town like mine. When I had moved to the school everyone knew my Snapchat account before my first day, yet, those personal questions about Allie were never answered.

April winds had just begun when the yellow scarf made its first appearance. Whether it was wrapped around her lush ponytail, tied on her bag strap or worn like a shawl it was always with her. So I thought nothing of it when she turned up one day with the scarf around her neck. Of course, I had my queries, like why she wore it in forty-degree weather, but I shrugged them off. Soon she wore the scarf around her neck every single day.

Another three months passed before our eyes locked again, however, this time I noticed change within her. Her bright, lively eyes had turned grey from forlornness. When she smiled, it was forced. As she walked away with her head down she clenched the tail of her scarf. I didn't think to ask her if she was okay.

Her friends eventually grew distant. I wasn't sure if it was mutual or because Allie had pushed them away. Once, I passed her when she was alone underneath the school's sycamore tree, but she felt unapproachable, different to the Allie I had met six months prior.

That sycamore tree became Allie's place. Even when winter arrived, she sat there at lunch while everyone else sat in the heated cafeteria. I would watch her twirl the tail of her scarf in her fingers. I don't think I saw her eat once.

The more I watched her, the less I talked about her. I knew people would think I was infatuated and judge me. I knew my parents would want to invite her over for dinner so they could interrogate her. I was embarrassed about my feelings and thought I'd be better keeping them to myself.

As the next school year arrived and the sycamore tree grew lush, I saw Allie less and less. It started with her missing last period, but it eventually grew to her leaving during lunch.

The sycamore tree looked bare without her sitting beneath it.

About five months into the next year our eyes met for the last time. While on my way to band lesson, I noticed soft crying coming from the girls' toilet. My instincts guided me straight towards it.

I opened the door a fraction and peeked inside.

Allie was curled up with her back to the wall. Tears stained her face and despondency drained her until she was weak. The songbird I once knew looked like it had all its beauty beaten out. Then I saw her eyes. Bloodshot. Soulless. Heavy. I desperately wanted to say something, but I didn't know what. I felt useless, out of place. So I turned and left.

That night, instead of sleeping, I thought of Allie. I thought about the tears she shed, the way her clothes didn't fit her anymore and the way she dug her nails into her leg when I peeked into the toilets. It felt like she was trapped in a different world, one which I couldn't understand. I wanted to reach out to her but doing so was more complicated than I had anticipated.

The next morning started ordinary but ended the opposite. On my way to school, I passed the town's park. Police cars lined the street, blue and white checker tape surrounded the park's largest oak tree and police officers were interviewing civilians. Worry sunk into me like a knife.

Jumping over the tape I sprinted towards the crime scene. Police officers chased after me, yelling and threatening me to stop but it only made me run faster.

When I reached the tree my jaw dropped. Laying on a bed of leaves was Allie, cold, pale and with the yellow scarf strangling her broken neck. 'Kid, you can't be here,' a middle-aged policeman stated sternly but then hushed because of how I looked at her. 'Did you know her?' I nodded slightly as my body tensed. 'I'm sorry for your loss. It's a horrible thing, suicide.'

It was gut-wrenching to look down at a frozen corpse and know what it looked like when it was lively and cheery.

I walked out of the park with a heavy heart. I kept my focus on the ground, I couldn't stand the sight of the trees. They reminded me of the songbird which sang no longer. Then, the sound of weeping met my ears.

An exhausted, distraught, fragile woman weeping into a tissue sat before me. She paused, her grey, weathered, sunken eyes turned towards me. Her dark, virgin hair was tangled and her jaw quivered. On her wrist was a bold tattoo which read '*Allie*'. My tears couldn't be held back any longer.

Only when I reached the point of no return did I realise my mistakes. I should have done something, but I didn't, and in the end that was what defined me.

BETRAYAL

LG Dalton

Michael sat back in the comfortable lounge chair as the waitress placed the tray of tapa dishes on the table before him. With an expert twist she popped a champagne bottle's cork, poured a glass, then placed the bottle in the ice bucket to his side.

'Luce will be with you soon,' she announced. 'He says you are to enjoy.'

'Does he now?' Michael muttered. 'Thank you, Lilith,' he called as the woman slinked back inside, sliding closed the glass doors to the balcony. 'Luce, huh?' His head moved in slight deprecation. He abhorred name shortening, but Lucifer was more lenient. He shrugged and sipped the champagne. Luce had an eye, and taste, for good food and better wine. It was one of his more irritating habits.

'What draws you from your lofty aerie, Michael?' Luce's mellow tones glided over Michael's nerves.

His gracile length flowed into the opposite chair. 'It is good to see you, old friend.'

'I heard you started a new business and decided to investigate for myself.' Michael examined the tray of dishes and selected the least innocuous looking. He smiled. As always, Luce emanated warmth and light.

'It is popular and profitable. Did you expect otherwise?'

'No. You have a good head for business.' He bit into the delicacy. 'The name is a little...' He swallowed, choked, and seized the glass of milk Luce obligingly handed him. He drained the contents and then glared at Luce. 'Juvenile,' he croaked.

'Your sense of humour hasn't changed,' Luce remarked. 'The regulars christened that one *Hades Hell*. Drink your champagne,' he instructed kindly.

Luc leant back in his chair and gazed out over the parklands leading to the river's edge. It was a magnificent vista and this private balcony had an unobscured panorama out to the bay islands. Kat, Dana and Ariel chose well when they selected the land and the architect. A quick deep breath and the tang of salt air filled his lungs. His gaze wandered back to his old friend.

'What muses you so?' Michael husked.

'You wouldn't understand. So what do you think of the name?'

'*Abbadon's Joy* is a little overdone for the ones who know.' He glanced at the blackboard menu implanted in the table. Luce loved technology. 'So are the dish names.'

'Try the one on the green plate. It is much milder and more your palate. Kat thought them up,' Luce admitted. 'I judged them apt and poetic.'

'You like her.'

'I liked her mother, too,' Luce retorted. 'How's the Old Man?'

'He misses you,' Michael remarked, selecting and devouring another tapa. For once he was thankful someone else introduced the topic. 'What went wrong between you?'

'Michael, Michael, Michael,' Luce sighed in the same tone and manner of an exasperated mother. 'You didn't understand then and you won't now.'

'Try me,' Michael retorted. 'It went deeper than a minor infraction.'

'Is that what he called it?'

'No. It is what I called it. It sounded more mature than disobedience.'

'You and Kat have a nice turn of words in common.'

Michael sipped his champagne and waited, refusing to take the Kat bait. He had patience down to an art. So did Luce. When they were younger, Luce was more impetuous, his energy as boundless as the sun's, with a love for life and all it entailed. However, the last altercation between Luce and the Old Man proved irreconcilable. He would like to see the rift healed. Why couldn't Luce swallow his pride for once? He used the table's touch screen for more tapas and champagne.

Luce's mouth twitched as Lilith slid a new tray of tapas onto the table, and left the opened champagne in the ice bucket. As the door opened and closed silently, Michael heard the late night crowd revving up. He was on his fourth glass of champers, and fifth tray of tapas.

'Forget about getting me drunk,' Michael told him. 'Like you, I may as well be drinking water. I am still waiting, Luce.' Sitting on this balcony watching the sun set and the stars rise was a delightful way to waste time. Luce was no slouch though. He owned strings of diverse businesses across the globe. This bar and nightclub was the latest acquisition.

'Tell me, Michael, why did you bow before the man?'

'Because I was asked to. Is that what this is about? Acknowledging a lesser being?'

'No. I acknowledge lesser beings and honour them for themselves all the time. It is about betrayal of the deepest kind.'

Michael blinked at him. The tapas remained untouched and the champagne went flat. 'How?' he asked at last. 'You helped conceal Kat, and then you disobeyed an order.'

'Leave Kat out of this. I refused to break a vow,' Luc corrected. 'The Old Man had no right to ask it of any of us.'

'Luce, he is the supreme commander. It is his right to demand anything he likes of us.'

'He has no right to demand we break a vow freely given to him, and every right to protect said vow with *his* life, and help us to keep that vow,' Luce seethed before he took a deep breath and closed his eyes.

'Your arrogance...'

'Arrogance?' Luc raged. 'Where is the arrogance in keeping a vow? Of helping and supporting others to keep their oaths? To this day we have not forsaken our covenant.'

Michael stared at his impassioned friend, gratified the glass walls soundproofed the balcony. The passion and temper of their youth was surging out of control. Luce always felt things deeply, but this went deeper. He often suspected the rift between Luce and the Old Man was rooted in more than simple disobedience and insubordination, but this revelation rocked the foundations of his beliefs, principles and commitments. He tilted his head and heard the faint rumble of rolling thunder. In a cloudless sky, it meant one of two things... and he liked neither scenario.

Luce drew a deep breath. He stared at the restless water, synchronising his breathing to its rhythm. His shoulders rose and fell, and his hands fisted and unfisted.

From beneath the balcony, laughter floated upwards. Its existence was a boorish obscenity against his abraded sensibilities. A flashing light caught his attention. Someone had superb timing or a death wish. Either way, someone was going to be worse for wear in the morning. He rose and left Michael to his thoughts.

Michael listened to the silence and heard glass breaking, a muffled yelp followed a thud, and invective flowed over raucous laughter. Luce's crisp voice silenced the protestor with succinct comments. The purr of a vehicle ended the contretemps. Luce reappeared at Michael's side, straightening his cuffs and jacket. 'Problem solved?' he asked.

Luce shrugged. 'For the moment. It comes with the establishment. People are gluttons many times over.'

'You should have named it something else.'

'Why? Human nature tends to the vices with little prodding.'

'You have no shame?'

'Shame for what?' Luce ran a finger across the onyx table top, revealing the security camera feed. He focused it on a table in the restaurant. 'This couple is enjoying a pleasant drink and time together. It is her birthday, and he budgeted for this evening. They will stay another hour and then go home and spend the rest of the night in each other's arms.' The feed spun to another couple. 'These two are regulars. They will drink too much and stagger home, but cause little trouble. They will sleep tomorrow away.' A swipe of a hand and a group of middle-aged businessmen appeared. 'These men are supposed to be formulating a joint business plan. In reality, they are looking for ways to sink each other, and walk away with their fortune. They are working on a quick-rich-scheme.' Luce circled with his finger and the scene spun. 'This male is drinking far too much, eating far too much, and stripping every woman under the age of forty naked with his gaze. You will notice only Lilith serves him. She has some creative torments in store for him. This group is celebrating the end of semester. You see they are merely drinking that awful cola drink, and chatting. '

'And the earlier altercation?'

'Contained. Mammon dealt with it. He is enjoying himself.'

'Why don't you contact the Old Man? I am sure he would like it.'

Luce stared out into the distance. As Kat said, his conscience was clear, regardless what people may think to the contrary. The Old Man was well aware of his activities. They may not communicate directly with each other, but they were well aware of the other's activities. They used many back channels and indirect methods. It was tiring and frustrating, but workable.

'I know he would,' he growled at last. 'Leave it alone, Michael. Just accept the situation as we have done.'

'It hurt you.' Michael grappled with the dawning realisation and sighed with heavy comprehension. He hated when others forced him into facing facts he had swept under the carpet. He sipped his champagne.

Luce was as silent as he sipped his wine. Michael preferred the French Champagne, but he preferred the crisper Australian wines. There was boldness about them, and the hint of warmth edged with ice shone through. The overconfidence of youth striding towards adulthood with all youth's inherent joy, eagerness, and audacity permeating the wine reminded him of his own youth.

Was arrogance his past or current sin? He was proud of how his people still fulfilled their covenant. Was it so wrong to be gratified in helping people strive to be their best? The students and married couple were the joys of this evening. Tomorrow they would go about their daily lives and tonight would be a fond memory in years to come. Was it erroneous to help them celebrate a life milestone?

Was it perverse to deliberately place temptation under people's noses? Everyone had the right of free will and free choice. The drunks could stop drinking at any time. Kat insisted on the local liquor laws being upheld, so Lilith and Mammon would stop serving them and call taxis. The kitchen shut down at midnight though some dishes were available until closing time. The gluttons could stop eating at anytime. The local food bank took the unused dishes and distributed it to the needy in the morning. Dana had a good network and insisted on telling the driver where to go so the food got to the right people. He thought about the note he found pushed beneath the front door. Laboriously scribbled and misspelt as it was, the emotions of the writer had shone through. Why should he be shamed for using the foibles of some to assist others in life? He thought it was a fair bargain and trade-off.

Did Michael ever consider the other side of the ledger sheet? As a general, Michael had few equals, but did he ever consider the price his opponent might pay? To him battle was less about reason and more about strategy and tactics.

Their battle was not about disobedience, or the desire to usurp the Old Man, but the refusal to forgo vows and oaths. It was a facet of the argument Michael never considered. Who was right? Or were they both wrong? Would Michael ever reconsider and let the past rest? Asking him to concede and accept a truce would be asking the impossible. There were topics on which Michael was as inflexible as Uriel. The difference between the two generals was Michael's methodical, systematic analysis combined with a flash of intuition.

Lucifer's shoulders bowed under the weight of the dilemma. He could only repeat what he knew. To have obeyed a direct order and bowed to Adam would have been a betrayal of his vow to never put another before God.

SLAYING OF THE GREEN-EYED MONSTER

Elizabeth Klein

Tuesday

A single envelope in the mailbox, more mail than I've received in a fortnight. It's probably a bill, or rubbish—don't expect any personal mail. It's a letter from my real estate agent, Jason. My rent has probably increased, or he's terminating my lease. I head upstairs to my tiny, single bedroom unit that overlooks a busy street.

The only thing of interest is the people who walk past. I love watching them from my window and make up stories about who they are and what they do during the day.

A maroon Alpha purrs by beneath my window. I crane my neck to see who it is. I've seen that car before and today, I'm given a brief viewing of its driver. A woman climbs out to dispose of a plastic bag in the skip. Her neat black hair shines in the fading afternoon sunlight; not a strand out of place. Such perfect rosebud lips and petite, size eight figure. Hip-hugging, leather skirts are not a problem for someone like her.

I mix Baileys and milk and pop a couple of chocolates into my mouth—a favourite pre-dinner snack. I'm still watching the woman. She's checking a broken fingernail. It's strange what you think about when you're watching people. I imagine her doing a photo shoot at a boutique studio somewhere in the city, modelling for the cover of an exclusive magazine. Swimwear, wide-brimmed hats with broad ribbons and floral stilettoes. Slim and sexy.

I catch a glint of green eyes in the sideboard's glass.

The woman slides into the leather seat of her car and it hums past my window to the back terraces where it's quiet and leafy. Where doctors and accountants live. She and her husband must have bought one of those three-bedroomed units with a pool. He's tall, incredibly cute with blond hair and has the body of Adonis. They're made for each other. It won't be long before I make myself known to her.

People arrive home. When you live alone, you become aware of all their noises. Cupboard doors slam upstairs, someone's talking loudly on the phone in the unit below me, a flushing loo echoes somewhere else. I switch off and try and concentrate on the work I've brought home. There's lots of maths and narratives to correct; it'll be a late night. Maybe I'll just make a sandwich and eat the rest of that chocolate in the fridge. I wander into the bedroom and wriggle out of the size eighteen skirt that was cutting into my waist and tie on a sarong instead. I'm able to breathe again.

The telly goes on, softly, though loud enough to hear human voices. My mind drifts. To fun-filled college days, basketball comps and long bike rides in the country with Geoff. That hidden scar lies deep. It's still raw and weeping after all these years. Dreams of a life together fade into the present solitude. His house is off limits. His wife, Cheryl, is too. My mind is tangled together with frayed string that might snap if I think about them for too long. Geoff and I were once college sweethearts. We lived together for almost three years while we studied. We did everything together—*everything!*

Green eyes flash and I hear a snarl. Ah, the evil inside us longs to escape.

Wednesday

It's such a relief to be home. It's not that I want to be here either, but I don't particularly want to be at work. No matter where I am, I feel empty, but I'd rather be at home, staring at the people in the street, wondering what they're up to rather than sitting in that sauna.

While I'm at the mailbox, the maroon Alpha pulls up. My heart leaps like I've swallowed a demented grasshopper. The size eight woman gets out and walks demurely to unlock her mailbox. Such grace. Even from where I stand, I notice things. Her sidewards glance at me. Ivory-skin, high cheek bones, close-fitting pants and low-cut blouse. I glimpse cleavage. Such a beauty.

Green eyes glare—*at her.* My heart races with possibilities.

I want to say hello, diffuse the tension, but by the time I'm ready to say something, she's already climbing into her car. But she *did* notice me. Hurt, I imagine a story to compensate. She's running late for a modelling shoot. Or perhaps she and her husband are eating out tonight at one of the local restaurants. In my mind, I see them holding hands as they stroll to the Italian, where he pulls out the chair for her to sit on before he slides in opposite. They're so in love! It's positively hateful!

Thursday

The red bead in the thermometer inches upward, pressing the high thirties. My damp undergarments stick to my hot thighs and breasts. My wet hair drips perspiration onto the kids' already grubby pages. I'm desperately trying to decipher the alien writing and make sense of squiggly lines and indiscriminate grammar so I can drive home, but my eyes sting from sweat. I end up shoving all the books into my bag. Marking at home is an innocuous pattern I'm familiar with. I walk to my Corolla baking in the hot, unforgiving sun behind the brick building. There's no air conditioning in it and it's a thirty-minute drive home. I long for a shower and a cold drink.

But I've learnt the dutiful rhythm of this cathartic existence. The futility of it all settles upon my soul and I close my eyes. Patience. If I let the sadness in, it'll swell into something huge and monstrous, morphed with black memories. Shameful acts I recall in snatches of screams and heartfelt pleas.

Avoiding the green-eyed monster, I hurry to my car, lugging the bag of books.

At home, I peel off my clothes, one soggy layer at a time and drink a can of cold lemonade from the fridge. My weeping mascara looks like moist, black bruises under my eyes. After a cool shower, I spill the bag of books over my dining-room table and stare at them with loathing. There's also the local newspaper and two overdue bills waiting to be opened. Before I retrieve another lemonade, the newspaper headline catches my eye: *Killer Still At Large.* I'm compelled to read on. My heart pounds as the words seep into my soul. Tonight, it feels as black as obsidian.

A second woman was discovered dead in her inner-city apartment. The police are hunting for her murderer.

Maybe I should lock my door. The green-eyed

monster shakes its head and licks its long pink tongue. Guess it wants some fun tonight. My heart pounds with excitement.

Thursday

The thermometer was nudging thirty-seven degrees. Monica turned up the air con in her Alpha and drove to the mailbox and at once wished she hadn't. Standing there was that frumpy, middle-aged woman again, this time with mascara running half-way down her cheeks. Her puffy face looked ghastly and long strands of wet hair were plastered to her sweaty cheeks and forehead. Guess the poor thing was just hot.

Thankfully, Monica's job as Chief Editor of one of Sydney's top fashion magazines meant she didn't ever have to leave her cool, plush office that overlooked the Harbour foreshore. Long lunches with clients in the restaurants below and lazy afternoons in the lounge were often prerequisites to successful modelling deals. Such a good life.

Monica didn't want to check her mail while that woman was there. She waited in the car for her to leave before she unlocked her mailbox. After slipping six scented envelopes into her handbag, she drove back to her lock-up garage. Monica couldn't wait to kick off her stilettoes and slip into something more comfortable. A quick shower and a glass of champagne while she waited for Pete, her latest boyfriend. She was looking forward to being taken to the theatre, followed by drinks at one of the exclusive clubs in the city.

In the shower, Monica thought about that strange woman at the mailbox. She's so uncouth, so banal! Probably works in some factory packaging dog biscuits. It would explain the state of her clothes, hair and face. *Arrgh*–that face!

I shouldn't be so unkind. But there was something hideous about it, and that stare she gave me.

For a moment, Monica stroked her soft hair, examining its length in the gilt-edged mirror in the bathroom. *Needs a cut. Maybe on the weekend.*

Just then, the doorbell rang.

Must be Pete. She glanced at her watch. *Gosh, he's early!*

She left her unit door ajar before she pressed the button that opened the downstairs security door. She could hear it open from where she was standing. *I'll wait till he knocks.* Unbuttoning her top button to maximise her cleavage, she waited near the door. The lingering seconds teased. She frowned. *Surely he's inside by now.* Monica opened the door.

That was when the screaming began.

Police are still on the hunt for an unknown killer of three women. Each were stabbed to death in a vicious attack in their suburban homes...

OVERRIDE

Nyssa Baschel

Römerberg, Germany 2085

The crunch of fresh snow under Aoibheann's heat absorbent boots gave her a false sense of security in Römerberg's bleak winter streets. Darkness had descended over the city square, illuminated by faerie-lights hanging from the traditional German eaves. She squinted through the sleet at an old man in a dark overcoat sitting on a park bench. His black Panama hat shielded his expression but in her mind she saw the wrinkle-lines etched across his narrow face and those steel blue eyes. It had been a decade but still, the thought of seeing him made her sick. But he was the closest thing she had to a father and if anyone could save her, he could.

He looked up from under the rim of his hat, smiling broadly. 'Aoibheann.'

Her jaw ached from clenching too tight and her

ribs throbbed from last night's attack but she fared better than her assailant.

'Call them off, Quinn.' She forced herself to sit next to him, staring into the crowd as they sung Christmas carols.

'Come quietly and they'll be called off.'

She turned to meet his cold stare. Her mouth went dry, seized by a memory.

Dr Quinn held her close, his whiskey breath made her sick as his greedy lips gorged at her mouth. He clutched at her backside and pulled her towards the hard lump in his pants. There was no escape that night, or any other night.

Tearing her glare from his, her heart raced. 'You owe me,' she said, fighting the urge to vomit, 'I was eleven, you bastard.'

'You're a cyborg—a hominoid nervous system genetically spliced with animal senses in a cybernetic case.'

His words crashed down on her, throwing her into turmoil as they always did. Aoibheann couldn't look at him. 'I dream, I feel, I think—' the image of Tobias flashed before her, *and I love.*

The old man shifted his weight and hardened his tone. 'Turn yourself in and Novatelas's troops will disappear.'

She clutched the bench underneath her thighs. 'They won't kill me?'

Quinn sighed. 'You harboured Tobias **Kühn**, a terrorist from the United Human Rights Alliance.'

She forced herself to meet his steel gaze. 'You

said I was special, that I would give Novatelas the cutting edge in reconnaissance—a strategic necessity. But this enemy you seek strives for justice. Sorry for my lack of *insight* but Novatelas has never given me anything to believe in.'

'Your circuits have been exposed to propaganda.' Bitterness usurped his tone.

'Circuits?' She spat back. 'Being molested by a corporate company is abuse no matter how you justify it, Tobias told me.'

Quinn's eyes narrowed. 'Do you think he wouldn't terminate you if he knew what you were?'

Her breath caught in her throat. 'I should kill you here.'

He didn't even flinch. 'You can't. Sensory Aggregate Programs disengage before they can kill a person. I came to see if your program could be repossessed—' he seemed to say more to himself than to her, '— but the corruption is too extensive.'

She searched his stare. *So that's it? You're going to let them kill me?*

He rose from the bench, straightening his overcoat. His aftershave assaulted her, reminding her of no escape.

'Time is of the essence,' he said flatly, 'Turn yourself in.'

Aoibheann turned to face the statue, Gerechtigkeitsbrunnen, proudly declaring a set of scales in the square's centre. Flashes of past missions spun in her head.

A girl watches in horror as a bullet shatters her

skull. Novatelas wanted to destroy what was in her head—A man's scream sends electric shocks through her spine as his wife's head topples to the ground. He had refused Novatelas—High pitched screams rise above the flames of the imploding thirty story apartment building. It looks good in the papers, Quinn said.

'I'm becoming human,' she whispered, but Quinn had already disappeared into the hoards. His smell and the sound of his raspy breath lingered in her supersonic senses long after he was gone.

Maybe I should turn myself in. Maybe falling for Tobias was just a glitch in the program. Maybe—

A scream shattered the chorus of Christmas carols, reverberating through Aoibheann's spine. Everything inside her recoiled, making her clutch her ears and squeeze her eyes shut. *They wouldn't dare kill me here.* Her throat tightened. But then again why not, she was just a failed program.

Shifting her awareness to sonar, she sensed the heavy boots that pound against the snow and the familiar metallic pang of machine guns. She leapt from the bench and shoved through the sea of fur coats and woollen hoods towards a hotel. *I have to find Quinn and force his hand. I'll make him file for special exemption from termination.*

She broke into a sprint as she reached an alley between two buildings. In the darkness she saw everything; mice scuttling across the ice, bags of trash piled next to dumpsters, a broken chair perched against the wall. Everything except Quinn.

A fresh onslaught of screams echoed through the sleet as the carols subsided. She sensed the first reactions of shock as confusion swelled through the crowd. The mass-flurry of pounding hearts threatened to overwhelm her. People pushed and shoved, creating a hysteria that made it hard for her to defend against sensory overload. She had to get out of there.

'There she is,' a silhouette yelled in German from the end of the alley.

Aoibheann pivoted into a crouch and scanned every contour of the trooper's face using the ultraviolet light spectrum. She downloaded it from her mind and sent it through to the *United Human Rights Alliance* database, an ability she acquired the last time she saw Tobias.

The memory of Tobias's stoic glare seized her, stealing precious seconds. Tears blurred her night-vision. *If only…*

'Stop,' yelled another Novatelas agent.

She wanted to send through other images but there was no time. Diving under a round of bullets, she somersaulted towards a uniformed man clutching a submachine gun. Her boot met his chin, sending him flying into the hotel wall. Aoibheann grabbed the gun and bolted around the corner, sensing the ground tremble under the boots of the approaching Novatelas paramilitary. Blood surged through her temples, her superhuman senses alert.

A vivid memory besieged her, making her double over. – *'You are everything Aoibheann.'*

Quinn whipped her fringe from her tear-drenched cheeks. 'You are a gift to the Free Nations.'

The stench of his aftershave lingered hideously in her nostrils as she struggled to gain control. Confusion washed over her, Novatelas was the only family she had known.

Shots echoed through the frosty alley, sending bolts of electricity through her body. Aoibheann pushed herself up from the snow and forced her legs run and leap over broken disregarded furniture. Behind her, the troops slowed as they scuttled over debris.

She broke out of the alleyway and darted towards Kaiserdom Cathedral. *Tobias said there was an underground porthole here somewhere.*

She threw her senses wide, risking being swamped by the human frenzy in the square, and the city's underground electric grid appeared beneath her. Luminescent blue lines buzzed painfully underfoot. It never really went away but when she tuned in it was worse - *a lot worse.*

Aoibheann winced at the throbbing that hammered her calves and thighs. Troops broke out of the alley as she darted towards huge stone arches. Bullets sprayed around her. She dove behind an arch pillar to catch her breath as the German voices shouted in pursuit.

Run, screamed the voice from within.

Without warning, powerful arms seized her from behind. She stopped her scream as memories of Quinn ricocheted through her mind. The arms tightened their grip, pulling her close. Aoibheann kicked out at the dark figure clad in licroid, a fibre that had hid his bodily functions from her senses. She writhed frantically but he was too close for her to get a clear kick or punch. Novatelas's troops were moments away. She couldn't get a glimpse of her captor. *Was he United Human Rights Alliance or Novatelas?*

She took a chance. 'Novatelas—they're here,' she panted, hoping he would release her enough for her to get a swing under his jaw. Her abductor said nothing. The warmth of his breath brushed against her cheek. Was he going to restrain her until the troops got here only to assassinate her? Of course, they wouldn't call it assassination; they'd call it 'terminating a program' as if pressing a delete button.

The man shuffled behind a stone pillar, pulling her with him. She sunk close into the man's embrace and Cathedral's shadows as the troops scuttled past.

Eternity could have passed before the footsteps disappeared and she was left with her heart beating against her assailant's forearm, waiting for the inevitable knife to be thrust under her ribs or the silent bullet to pierce the back of her head.

'Aoibheann,' the familiar German voice whispered in her ear.

'Tobias?' She spun around.

His eyes searched hers before his warm lips enclosed her mouth, leaving her to wonder if he knew she was the one who led Novatelas to him a month ago.

She had to face it. Honesty was the only way between them. 'I'm sorry.'

Sadness fell over his gaze. 'It wasn't your fault. You had to.'

'You... know? And you forgive me?'

'Of course.' He kissed her again. 'But the others don't.'

Aoibheann touched his jaw with her fingertips; no one had ever had her back. But the ultimate lie hung between them. It always would. 'We need to get out—'

'No, this way,' he whispered, pulling her towards an arched wooden door with an iron lock. 'Work your magic.'

She cringed. Picking locks was a cyborg ability. 'Why do you think—'

'Surveillance cameras.'

Her stomach dropped. It was only a matter of time before he discovered what she was. *He'll hate me*. A lump stuck in her throat. *Actually, he'll kill me*.

'Come on,' he whispered.

She resisted. 'Why?'

'You'll see.'

Aoibheann heard the beat of his heart; it was fast but nothing unusual under the circumstances. She couldn't tell if she could trust him.

Yells in the distance told her the troops were coming back. She broke from his embrace and faced the cathedral door. Standing between his view and the lock, Aoibheann slid out a metal key pick from the top of her hand and jerked the lock sideways. With a click it gave and she flicked it away, edging the door open. Tobias threw her wry grin as he slid past and led her down a dim corridor. She couldn't read sincerity behind the expression.

'Careful,' he whispered. 'These stairs are uneven.'

She suppressed the urge to laugh; she has night sight, he doesn't know after all.

Aoibheann shadowed Tobias through the archway into a back room. The only window was high above. Frosted glass clouded the moonlight. Several familiar faces stared at her—men of the *United Human Rights Alliance.* Consciously she slowed her breath and strolled between them, following Tobias towards a lump under a woven hessian blanket. He threw the blanket off a writhing figure who glared up at her from swollen eye sockets.

'Quinn,' the name slipped from her lips.

Quinn flinched, narrowing his eyes and shifting his weight.

'I didn't want to rob you of the honour,' Tobias whispered, 'Payback.'

The hideous laugh that came from Quinn echoed through the chamber. In the dark, she saw the mockery play in his steel blue eyes.

'Kill me, Aoibheann,' he croaked through a

twisted grin.

Her heart skipped a beat. She wanted to, she really wanted to; and not just to keep her lie. Aoibheann stepped forward, acutely aware of Tobias handing her a metal pole. She took the weapon, skilfully twirling and considering her next move. Everyone would know what she was if she failed. She had to override Novatelas' safety valve in her brain.

Aoibheann raised the pole; *I'm as free as any human! I can choose my actions.*

Quinn's eyes widened. She slammed the pole down – and the room went black.

'Aoibheann.' She awoke to Tobias's voice.

Her eyes darted around the room, there was no one else there. Had Quinn escaped?

He stared at her, propping her up from behind. 'What happened?'

'I—' tears blurred her vision. She pushed them back, strengthening her resolve. 'Where's Quinn?' *I have to kill him.*

'Anton's on to it,' he said slowly, studying her.

'I'll do it,' Aoibheann declared dragging herself up.

Tobias grabbed her arm. 'Wait.'

Aoibheann's autonomic reaction took over and she spun into a somersault and landed on her feet by the door. She pivoted towards him. 'I—' *have no excuses left.*

'Cyborg,' he mouthed, stepping back wide-eyed.

Aoibheann wanted to deny it, expecting a bullet in her chest. But he didn't raise his gun.

Damn, there's no time.

Aoibheann turned and raced down the corridor, clutching the metal pole. Death would be bearable if she took Quinn out first. She had to take control, show herself as human. She would force herself to override Novatelas' circuitry.

Switching to heat detection, Aoibheann located Quinn a floor below. Anton was not far behind, but Quinn had found his way under a pile of straw in a storeroom. She bolted down stone spiral stairs and through the underground corridor, turning a corner no one else had seen. Not stopping to think, she belted the straw with the pole. Quinn let out a cry and she sensed the other's turn back towards them.

Flashes of Quinn's predatory night games seized her. She let the visions fuel the anger to override the blackness threatening to consume her consciousness and whacked the straw over and over again. Finding his head with x-ray vision, she smashed the pole into his skull – the room turned black.

She had no idea how long she had stood there, frozen. The straw had turned red and it had given way to expose Quinn's hazy eyes.

'How?' Quinn mouthed through blood.

She circled the bloody pole through the air, 'I told you, I'm becoming human,' and she bought the final blow down on his head. The crack of his skull filled the chamber, as she realised there was something satisfying about watching fear flicker in his dying eyes.

Shuffling boots alerted Aoibheann and she turned.

Tobias stood in the darkness. She saw his mouth ajar with ultraviolet clarity. His whisper was too soft for the others entering from the corridor to hear. 'No human syndicate will accept you.'

'Maybe,' Aoibheann whispered back, a sense of power solidifying within.

Lethal tension lingered between them.

Aoibheann strode over to him, ignoring him flinch as she touched his jaw. 'The real question is do *you* accept me?' she whispered into his ear, 'After all, you should be the first to admit humanity made me in their own image.'

GALLERY, 3

E J A

The manic draws on the wall, never knowing, never guessing he found something that could change the world, because his mind broke with his heart a long time ago.

The Sight

Fiona Emily

She moves. One moment her eyes are closed. Her head down on the table with strands of dark hair tangled across her face. The next she jolts upright. Lanky limbs shift from sitting to standing, so fluidly it's graceful. Moving in ways that surprise me, no matter how many times I've watched her before.

As she tucks her lunchbox then textbooks into her bag, she wears this expression – her lips partly drawn, her gaze introspective. A look I've seen on her numerous times, but it always conjures the same feeling.

A longing that should not be present.

What is she thinking?

Clutching the branch above me, I tell myself I should move. Swing down from this tree and return home to the bottle of Jack Daniels with my name on it. Whatever brings me back here is foolishness . . . she's nothing to me. Just a girl, someone harmed by my wrongs yes, but nothing can be done to bring back the dead of this world. Watching her this way . . . only evokes emotions that have no place in my existence.

My fate was sealed with the death of her parents. The circumstances matter not . . . just the act itself which bound me to the depths of hell. Every time I visit the place with another soul, the shackles grow stronger, wrestling what's left of my heart, thieving away the remnants of my humanity.

Not that I had any to begin with.

I shift, planning to drop to the ground, when her gaze flicks up beyond the building. Scanning the trees. Watchful. Wary. Like she knows I'm here. Which is impossible . . . I'm unseen. Unknown. Part of the shadows.

Slinging her bag over a shoulder, she turns and marches inside. I shift at once, not away like I should, but down to the ground, skirting the back of the building, to reach a better vantage point.

For this is my favourite part.

With her dinner break over she's back to work, entering the first room along the hall. The curtains are parted, providing perfect viewing as she reaches the presence in the bed. She speaks avidly to her unaware patient, making me wonder what her one-sided conversation could be about. My fixation moves from her lips to her hands as she tends with such care and attention, freely giving of dignity, without any consideration for if it's deserved.

All too quickly she's done and shifting to the next room.

She ducks into the hall out of sight. I creep to the next window, waiting restlessly for her to appear. Her silhouette materialises in the doorway. Fingers slide along the wall to the nob just inside the door, bathing the darkened room in soft light.

She doesn't move. Her entire body motionless except for her hand which drops from the switch. She's fixated on something. It's only when I shift my focus from her that I see the dark figure looming over the patient laid out on the bed.

I press my nose to the glass.

That's not just any figure. The black cloak unmistakable, along with the shimmer of other worldliness that comes from visiting the realms. A reaper? Here? In my territory? There's been no call to collect a soul, I would know if there was - and yet . . .

Wait. She's staring at him. Eyes full of confusion like she *sees* him.

Which is impossible.

Her lips move. The reaper's head flicks up. He stares at her, his focus no longer on the sorry soul in the bed, but on her.

She steps backwards. Reaches for a red fire extinguisher from the wall, heaving it up as though she intends to use it as a weapon. Which is ludicrous, she doesn't need a weapon, she's living breathing . . . the only thing to fear from a reaper is in death . . .

He steps towards her.

I move without thinking, diving through the window, using my cloak as a shield. The window shatters, showering the room in fragments.

She staggers back against the wall.

The reaper is no longer focused on her. Just the effect I wanted.

Yellow eyes stare me down. Cold and inhuman, a colour I've never seen in a reaper before, the sight gnawing in the pit of my stomach. I know at once this is no normal reaper. But something far far, worse.

'This is not your business,' he grunts without one blink of those stormy predator eyes. 'There is no soul here for you tonight.'

'And yet . . . here you are.' I examine the man on the bed behind him, the very one who was the subject of his attention not so long ago. Still alive, but weak. Was this reaper trying to take a living soul? One not yet deemed for collection? Such a path only leads to condemnation . . . I should know. Although the way his eyes burn like evil is aflame within, suggests he's way beyond that.

Which means *she* is even more at risk.

Fear is not something I've known in a very long time. I'm usually the one invoking it. But it's here now, prickling up my spine. Not for myself. But her.

'Leave. Before we have a problem,' I say, my voice a growl.

Unblinking he gazes upon her, ignoring my request, staring like she's a prize he intends to claim.

'She can see us,' he hisses his voice as slippery as a snake. 'Do you know what that means? She has ... the sight,' his face contorts with glee. His mind ticking over, assessing, pondering her uses. 'The rarest of gifts in a human - rather valuable might I say ... so we do indeed have a problem ...'

I'm still stuck on his ugliest of words. 'Valuable?' Rage eats out my insides. Rumbling up through my stomach, bringing with it an all consuming anger.

He has no idea of her worth. It comes from who she is, not because of some gift of sight. My greed for her only grows as I note the earnestness with which he wants her. She is mine. He will never have her. Never.

He attacks, nails poised like talons out to rip me apart. Using fists and forearms I deflect him. His nails gouge my skin, but I feel nothing even as blood seeps to the surface. I'm too incensed, overcome by a churning need to give back what I've received.

We stare each other down. He snarls, displaying a set of razor sharp teeth. It's meant to scare me. What he doesn't know is that I have a pent up storm of resentment within, unspent, just waiting for an outlet. For me, this is relief.

I bounce on my feet, eager for his next move. He dives at me. Ducking low, I go for his arm, heaving his bulk sideways up-ending him against a cupboard that rattles like it might fall.

Within seconds he's back on his feet, flying at me again. My body blocks him. I taste blood as his fists fly. It's motivation to ram him harder, driving him backwards with every grunt of effort until he crashes against the bed. He pushes back, forcing my boots to slide on the slick surface. I grab his cloak, yanking it down before slamming my fist in his face.

He staggers backwards, glaring at me. Astonished, annoyed, angry. Need still burns in those sickly eyes.

For her.

I glower back, making certain he knows my intent. He must see something he doesn't like for he shakes his head.

'This isn't over.' In one swift move he lunges away, one foot on the bed, one on the windowsill, disappearing into the dark of night.

I watch him go, uncertain, that fear still a palpable, growing unease.

Searching the room I look for her. She's huddled beneath a table, clinging to the red fire extinguisher. I crawl to her, checking her over at once, relief only allowing air to reach my lungs when I see she is unharmed.

She stares at me.

Sees me.

I back away, not wanting to crowd her, stretching to stand, so she can climb out from her hiding space. Broken glass covers the floor. Mess is scattered across the room.

Tentatively she stands, shaking, but managing somehow to hold it together even after what she just witnessed. Hands clasped on the fire extinguisher just in case.

'You're no guardian angel are you?' her voice warbles.

There's no white light for her, no warmth for her to feel, like the usual experience when I visit to collect a soul. Then again she is alive. Very much alive. And she *sees* me.

Her gaze begins at the tips of my jet black hair to the bottom of my scuffed boots. What she sees of my young human form, as rough as it is, is no true indication of what's within. The years have blurred. I'm weary, shackled to depths of darkness, my nature conformed to the ravages of hell that shall one day consume me as its collector. It's reaper.

'There are no guardian angels, only monsters who bring death.'

I expect her to back away. To be afraid.

If not from my words, then from the blackness in my soul.

'And yet you saved me,' she whispers, one trembling hand lowering the fire extinguisher to rest it on the ground, her gaze penetrating mine.

I'm entranced by the way her eyes examine me. Without an inkling of fear. Sure there's uncertainty. Confusion. But not fear. She even lowers her weapon as though she believes I am no threat. Like she sees something other than what I am.

She's wrong. So wrong.

What I could do to her if I pleased.

I back towards the window, needing to escape those probing eyes, her sight too uncomfortable.

The shadows beckon. I rush for the window, bursting out into the night. Returning to the familiar. The darkness. My footsteps halt when I hit the shadows. If only I could walk away and disappear into the night. Return to my bottle of Jack Daniels without a second thought. But I can't. Not now I know what's out there. Leaving was hard before, now it's impossible.

She might see, but she has also been seen - by something far worse than me, that before tonight I would not have thought possible.

What's done cannot be undone. Only defended.

I protect what's mine. And she will always be mine.

I take a deep breath and settle in.

It's going to be a long night.

THE VOICE

Jodie Lane

'Oh, Connor sleeps through, he's so clever.' The mum's voice is smug, at least in my ears. I don't hear the replies of the other mums in the group, but I know what they are thinking.

Look at that new mum. Look how tired she is. Her baby was crying when she came in. I bet she doesn't know what she's doing.

And they are right. I bite my lip in an effort not to cry. Stacey hates the car. She was screaming her head off when we arrived at the clinic.

Coming to this mums' group was a bad idea. I should have just stayed home and tried to get her to sleep.

But Stacey refuses to sleep in the cot. I do everything right; swaddle her, put her at the bottom of the cot on her back, shush her gently and rock the cot and she just screams and screams until

I can't take it anymore. I always end up picking her up and rocking her to sleep. Now after eight weeks the slightest cry puts my teeth on edge. Even when she finally sleeps I dread the moment she wakes.

I hate it. Everyone said how wonderful it would be. Hard but wonderful. But I hate it.

Stacey is due for a feed soon but she's fallen asleep my arms and there's no way I'm going to wake her. If I'm lucky I'll get her into the car and be able to race home, buying myself a few precious minutes of quiet.

Why do all these other mums look like they have it so together? I'm dying inside.

'Now make sure take to advantage of the services here at the clinic,' the child health nurse says. 'You can weigh bub, talk to our breastfeeding nurses, touch base about post-natal depression warning signs.'

I cringe at those words.

I can't be depressed. I'm smarter than that. I just have to keep going and tough it out. I don't need help. Don't want everyone to think I'm a failure.

The session ends. I rush out the door, cradling Stacey. My oversized nappy bag crashes into the doorframe. Reaching the car I turn the ignition, winding the windows down and blasting the air-con in an effort to cool the car.

'Hey, you've got a real cutie there.' One of the other mums—I can't remember her name—is parked next to me. Her little boy sleeps with his face smooshed on her shoulder, dark curly hair askew.

Shit. What's her name? God, I'm so hopeless.

'Thanks.' I try to smile. 'Your boy is gorgeous too.'

'Hey, do you have anywhere to be right now?' the woman asks. 'I don't really want to go home just yet, so wondered if you maybe wanted to grab a coffee? There's a shop just around the corner. If I put Lee in the car he's bound to wake up.'

Coffee? No, I should just go home. Can't afford coffee—we're on one income now.

'Um.'

'Please?' The woman smiles. 'I could really use the company, and you seemed nice in the group.'

Nice? I barely said a word. Didn't dare. I would have started crying. Barely holding it together now.

'I shouldn't,' I whisper.

'Coffee *and* cake?'

I give a half-hearted laugh. 'Oh, I better not. Trying to lose the baby weight and that.'

'Fuck that,' the woman says. 'Are you breast-feeding?' I nod. 'Then you need cake. You burn five hundred calories a day, and I don't know about you but when I'm up sixteen times a night I need frickin' coffee.'

'Um, okay.' I'm being weak. I should go home. Put Stacey in the cot. I have to train her to sleep or I'll go insane. But I turn off the car and follow the woman—*what's her name? God, I'm hopeless!*

'I'm really sorry,' the woman says when we reach the coffee shop. 'I've forgotten your name.

Brain like a sieve these days.'

The smell of roasted beans and warm milk soothes me and I giggle. I tell her my name. 'And this is Stacey. And, um, I've forgotten yours.'

'Kelly and Lee.' Kelly smiles and settles Lee onto her other shoulder.

'I thought it was just me,' I chuckle but then begin to cry. Great, fat tears roll down my cheeks and my body shakes. Stacey grizzles and I try to shush her but the sobs just turned into hiccups and my daughter scrunches up her face and wails.

'Hey! Hey!' Kelly reaches over and pats my shoulder. 'It's okay, hon.'

'I'm so sorry!' I wipe my nose with the back of my hand, repositioning Stacey in an effort to rock her back to sleep.

You loser! Oh, how fucking hopeless are you? Crying in front of a complete stranger, in the middle of a coffee shop.

Customers raise their heads like a field of cattle and stare. 'I should go.'

'Hey, no.' Kelly puts out her hand. 'Hey, can we sit up the back in a booth?' she asks the waitress. I allow myself to be led past all the grannies munching on scones and hipsters with their turmeric lattes. The hubbub of chatter drills into my mind, critical comments and judgemental glances. I sniff and nod when Kelly orders us both a flat white. 'Lactose free. And a slice of that carrot cake—two spoons. Thanks.'

It's feeding time. I pull up my shirt and balance a

nipple shield on one breast, struggling to guide Stacey's screaming mouth onto it without knocking it loose. Kelly notices.

'Oh, you're using shields? That's hard. You poor thing, tell me what's going on.'

'It's nothing. I'm sorry. I'm just a bit tired.'

So hopeless. Can't even keep it together at a coffee shop. Useless.

'Uh, duh you're a bit tired! Bet you haven't had a full night's sleep in months! I was a hippo at the end of my pregnancy—back ached and got up every half hour to pee! Sucks! Sleep deprivation is a killer, my friend. It messes with you big time.'

'I know,' I sniff. Stacey finally latches on and sucks with the fierce determination of a starving infant. 'I guess today was just a bit harder than normal. I try not to go out much.'

'Oh, honey.' Kelly reaches out, taking my hand this time. 'Does it make you anxious to go out? I was like that with my first kid. Barely left the house. Felt sick just thinking about it. Thought everyone was judging me and saying how hopeless I was. It was awful.'

I gaze at her through bloodshot, teary eyes. 'Really?' *It's not just me?* It's as though a fist around my heart unclenches ever so slightly.

Kelly laughs. 'I was a fucking mess. Ended up in sleep school, anti-depressants, seeing a shrink. Have to say though, the help I got was the best thing ever. I was in a bad way.'

Yes, but you're probably not a bad mother like I

am.

'How... how old is your first kid?'

'Savannah? Six. Couldn't handle the thought of another baby before then. Was so terrified I'd go off the deep end again. Still on the happy pills and still seeing a counsellor from time to time. It's good maintenance.'

How does she seem so together? How come I'm falling apart?

Our coffees arrive, along with the carrot cake. 'Dig in,' Kelly orders. 'You look like you need a treat.'

That starts the tears again. Stacey falls off and I bring her upright for a burp, hauling my shirt down. I curse at the milk that leaks through my bra. 'Shit, I forgot breast pads.'

'Don't stress, hon. No one is looking, and you've got a new baby so fuck anyone who dares to judge. Half the women have been there and we're on your side.'

Stacey burps and snuffles into my neck. I love the closeness but wish desperately I could just put my daughter down. 'I just feel so hopeless all the time. I knew it would be hard, but it's killing me. I'm scared I—' I stop.

Shit, what are you doing? You almost blurted out that you're a bad mother! Shut up!

Kelly looks at me, compassion in her eyes. 'You're scared?' she prompts gently.

Tears well up again. 'I'm scared I'm going to hurt her,' I whisper. 'I get so tired.'

Kelly nods. 'You're scared you're going to hurt her by accident? Or on purpose?'

She knows! She's going to report you or something! You aren't fit to be a mother!

Yet still the words creep out. 'On purpose...' I look at Kelly, expecting damnation. 'I'm such a bad mother.'

'Oh, my dear. You poor thing. You poor, poor thing. You're not a bad mother. The fact that you're scared of that means you're a good mother.'

I stare at her, confused. Kelly nods sadly. 'I was the same. I was so out of my mind with tiredness and anxiety I was terrified I would drop Savannah, or slap her, or deliberately knock her head against the doorway. I thought I was evil. But it wasn't me thinking that, not really.'

'Huh?' I bob Stacey up and down. She rewards me with another burp.

'It's an ego-dystonic thought. That's what my shrink told me. It's the manifestation of your worst fears. You see, a bad mother, or a bad parent, wouldn't care if they hurt their child. You want to protect them, even from yourself. That means you care about them.'

'Um, I suppose?'

Kelly sighs. 'Look hon, I know we've only just met but my heart is breaking for you because you are exactly where I was five years ago. Will you please come back to the child health clinic and talk to one of the midwives there. I'll stay with you if you like? Or I can piss off if you want privacy. But please, please, please don't just go home and stew on this. Your mind is working against you right now.'

'Oh, no, I should just go home!' Even as I say it, I feel sick at the thought. The empty house. The sink full of dishes and dirty washing staring accusingly. The crying baby. My loneliness.

'That's the anxiety talking.' Kelly stabs the carrot cake and eats some, waving the fork. 'It's fucking evil. I know I seem like I'm being the biggest busy-body but I would be the shittest person if I walked away right now. Please.'

I stare at her. Maybe she's right. Maybe I do need help 'Okay...' I rearrange Stacey to keep feeding and lean awkwardly to the side to drink my luke-warm coffee.

'Good girl,' Kelly says. 'Now eat some carrot cake. It's going to be okay.'

LIFE CHANGING

Nikki Lentfer

'There you are, you naughty boy.'

I took my cat out of her hands and shut the door. Then, remembering I should be polite, I opened it again and said, 'Thanks.'

The woman recovered her smile. 'Hi, I'm Julie,' she said. 'I found him on the road and I thought he might be yours. He seemed a little hungry so I fed him. I hope that is okay.'

'Sure,' I lied as I stroked my cat.

'I just love animals,' she said. She was so bouncy with happiness that her blonde ponytail bobbed up and down. 'I would be happy to feed him any time.'

That gave me an idea. 'Would you like to come in?' I said and put on a smile.

'I haven't got much time,' she said, but she came in.

It has been many years since anyone visited my house and I regretted it almost immediately. I could see Julie's hand creep up under her nose as she tried to act as if she hadn't noticed the smell.

I had forgotten about the smell. I didn't notice it anymore. 'Sorry, I think there is a sewage leak,' I said. She was a big girl. I wondered if she dieted.

I showed her into the living room where she sat on the edge of the couch looking awkward. I sat on a nearby easy chair facing her.

'You haven't told me your name,' she said, moving some clothes along the couch to get more comfortable.

'I'm Miriam,' I said. I wondered how long it had been since I had told anyone my name. How long since I had spoken to anyone other than the clerk at the grocery store? My life had become boring.

The cat jumped off my lap and up next to Julie. Julie reached out to tickle his ears. 'What is his name?'

'I call him Seven. I have other cats but he is my favourite.'

The smile wavered. 'Seven? Like the number? What an interesting name. Is there a reason you chose that name?'

I had to think fast. Tell or not tell? I decided to tell. There was no hurry. All I planned to do this afternoon was feed my cats.

'His name reminds me of a life-changing moment,' I said. 'A long time ago, I won two hundred dollars on a Lotto ticket. Money was tight, but I decided to spend it on a flight in a small plane. I had always wanted to fly.'

'How brave of you. Is that what changed your life?' asked Julie smiling widely.

'Not then,' I said. 'At the airport, I met Sergio. He had deep grey eyes and long curly lashes. He talked me into skydiving instead.'

'Skydiving. That is life changing.' Julie's perky voice was getting annoying.

'Oh no,' I said. 'When it was time to jump I couldn't do it. Sergio stayed with me and we flew back together. I fell in love with him.'

'Oh, how romantic,' said Julie as she looked around for a photo. I had none.

'Yes, romantic,' I continued. 'He made me pregnant and then left me to cope alone. My dad was angry, but my sister invited me to live with her.'

'That was nice of her,' Julie said with less bounce in her voice. I was tired of her interrupting. I gave her a look that would freeze burning coals. She looked stunned, then stood up with her keys in her hand.

'Please sit,' I said. She sat heavily on the edge of the couch again.

'Things were going well until I had the baby. She only lived for three days.'

Julie tried to look sympathetic but she just looked nervous. Her eyes kept darting to the door and back.

'My brother in law accused me of not taking care

of the baby properly.' Julie watched me, her eyes wide and glistening.

'That was the first time I had to stab someone,' I said.

Julie looked as if she might faint. She stood up, murmuring something and tried to act as if she just happened to be heading to the door. I let her go. I wasn't silly enough to have all my knives in the kitchen. I took the nice sharp hunting knife off the wall and followed her. There was no hurry. I had locked the door when she came in. Plus, I wanted to finish my story.

'And THAT was the moment that changed my life,' I said.

Julie knew the door was locked. She went left down the hall towards the cat's room. She was stumbling. Falling against the wall as if I had already stabbed her.

I let her go for a bit. I liked the chase part.

She opened the door and froze with her hand over her mouth. I crept up behind her but she didn't move. Even I was repulsed by the skull on the floor. The cats had made good work of it and it was almost picked clean. It was the last piece of my last visitor.

It was so nice of Julie to offer to feed my cats. I think that will be life-changing for her.

It will also be a change for my favourite cat. 'Come on Eight,' I said a few moments later. 'Let's go get some freezer bags.' And he came.

GALLERY, 4

EJA

We read love stories, we read fantasy, we read science fiction, and we wish the darkness of our lives to fade away like a magically healing scar. We wish we could have our friends' bright light, but they are just hiding their sadness like the moon hides the sun in a solar eclipse.

LOVE LETTER

Miriam McGoldrick

It's 5.00 pm, Friday. I turn off my computer.

What was it Marion asked me to do on my way home? Pick up something for dinner, post some letters or buy some wine? No, none of those. I check my wallet. Of course, the dry-cleaning voucher.

At the dry-cleaner's there's one person ahead of me.

A woman's voice calls, 'Rupe.'

I freeze. Feel as though I've been shot.

Again, she says, loudly, 'Rupe!'

I force myself to lift my head and look. There's a woman out the back, behind the lass at the counter. The woman's ironing a huge white table cloth. She stops, balances the iron on its heel on the ironing board and looks right at me. 'It is you, Rupe. After all these years.'

My tongue seems to be stuck to the roof of my mouth. I cough. It feels a lifetime since I heard that name. My heart pounds. 'You talking to me? You must be thinking of somebody else.'

I look at her again. Gorgeous legs. My God, it's Beryl. Sweet innocent Beryl who helped me lose my virginity. Unwillingly, my mind slips back. I worried about her for years.

Hell, now she's standing right next to me. Her hand is on my arm. 'Are you all right, Rupe?'

'I told you. You've got the wrong person.'

'I don't think so.'

She's still cute as a button but a lot older, a lot wiser.

'You see, I found this letter in your jacket pocket. Now, you wouldn't want that letter getting in to the wrong hands, would you? I mean, what would Marion say?'

'Sorry. You really have confused me with somebody else.'

'So, I'll keep it for her, will I? She said she'll be bringing in some blankets next week.'

'What letter? Are you trying to blackmail me?'

'Rupe, we're old friends', she says, obviously offended. 'I couldn't ask you for money. But your wife should know about that Madeline; I mean the one who wrote the letter. Funny, Marion and I are tuck shop buddies at the high school.'

'My wife and I don't have any secrets.'

'I don't understand why you're pretending to be somebody else. She says your name's Robert. So you're happy for me to give her the letter?'

'You might as well give her the jacket too.' I want to storm out the shop but am now so light headed that I walk slowly like an old man so I won't fall.

All these years and nobody's recognised us. Our move was very painful but the police promised it had a high chance of being successful. Part of me wants to go straight back and explain to Beryl that we had no choice.

We could have hung around in that little outback town after our daughter disappeared all those years ago. Word at the time was that I'd molested her and killed her to make sure she'd never tell. Despite the inquest, that sort of talk never stops. If we'd stayed, the story would have grown and grown.

The police warned us it'd be tough. They were wonderful and helped in so many ways. It meant a whole new identity for both of us in totally different circumstances. Nobody knows. We never had any more children. How could you risk having your children discover a secret like that? I'm sure that getting involved with the local P & C has helped Marion.

Bugger Beryl!

At home I pour myself a double scotch, clink in a couple of ice cubes then down it in almost one gulp; it burns and I feel slightly sick.

Marion looks at me. 'What the hell! Are you okay, love? You look as though you've seen a ghost.'

'You could say that.'

'Perhaps I'd better have a drink too. I'll pour you another one if you promise you won't skol it.'

I nod. I can't stop the tears coming. 'You know I love you madly.'

'Shh! You promised you'd never say that again.'

'Remember the night we went out for that special anniversary dinner?'

'Of course I do.'

'I told you then too that I love you madly.'

'And we came home and made wild passionate love.'

'It must have been the champagne.'

'And?'

'Remember that one letter? The letter from you that I just couldn't destroy?'

'Oh hell, Robert. Tell me the worst.'

'It was still in my jacket pocket and Beryl found it at the dry-cleaner's.'

'So the Beryl I know is the same Beryl you knew as a kid?'

'Apparently. Remember I told you she was my first girlfriend? Well, our parents were friends and her Mum and Dad showed up with her one night at our place. Beryl was pregnant ...'

'You mean the child was yours? How come you never told me?'

I shrug. 'I felt so sorry for Beryl. Mum was horrible to her, said she was a slut and the kid could have been anybody's. Anyhow, Dad gave them some money to help them move away. We never heard from them again.'

'You really care about her. Why didn't you ever tell me?'

'For years I thought we could have raised our child. I had my paper run and Beryl had shifts at KFC. Of course now I know it would have been silly.'

'Life's been so good here. We've been very careful. What are we going to do?'

'We'll have to get rid of her. And very soon.'

She punches me on the arm. 'Robert! You don't mean kill her?'

'Unless you can come up with a brighter idea.' I kiss her. 'We both know we can't ever go back to being Madeline and Rupert.'

'I suppose not. But I can't believe we're even talking about killing somebody.' She starts to cry.

'Marion, I'd never joke about anything like this. Don't you see? It's because of what we've been through…. Do you really think I don't remember how much the gossip and vandalism upset you? We agreed with the police nobody should ever know. By the way, didn't you say last night that we were going somewhere tonight?'

'Sure. The P & C Christmas Dinner's on. For goodness sake, Robert, you don't want to go out now after what you've just told me.'

'Will Beryl be there?'

'She's even made a new dress for tonight.'

'Mmm. It's the ideal opportunity.' I put my arm

around her. 'Calm down. It'll be fine. You'll see. Perhaps you should take one of your sedatives.'

'Good idea.'

'How many people are going to be there?'

'Let's say ten. They've had eight acceptances. What are you going to do, Robert?'

'You know that bottle of absinthe I gave you for your birthday?'

'You mean the weird stuff that looks like the cordial we called Green Death when we were kids?'

I laugh. 'That's right. Most people have never tasted absinthe. If we hurry, I'll make them all a fabulous cocktail each and with all the fancy carry on it'll be easy to pop something extra in Beryl's glass; that way we'll make sure she never wakes up.'

'What are you going to use?'

'Leave it to me. It's better you don't know. Don't worry, I'll slip a packet in her pocket or handbag. They'll think she accidentally took an overdose.' I kiss her. 'There's no other choice. We've got far too much to lose. Always remember, whatever happens, I love you madly.'

We dress quickly. I pop the bottle, sugar cubes, glasses and a couple of cards of tablets in a carton while Marion wraps our Secret Santa gifts.

At the party I pull an extra table out of the storage room, cover it with a white cloth and set out the glasses. I crush a few of the tablets while Marion circulates, asking everybody whether they'd like a cocktail.

Marion dims the lights. I pass my hand dramatically over the first glass, popping in the powder. Then I go through the whole ceremony of pouring the absinthe over the sugar cube and lighting it. I pass Marion the glass, 'Cheers, darling. Enjoy.'

I make six more cocktails and put them on a tray. As Marion picks up the tray I grab one of the drinks for Beryl and wink as I hand her the glass which she thumps down on the table before walking away.

Later, at home, I make Marion another spiked absinthe cocktail and hand her her sleeping tablets.

In the morning I check Marion's pulse. She's quite cold. I reach across her body for her mobile phone. I make the call, 'Hi Beryl. It's Rupe. Are you free for lunch today? What about the pub? I'm really looking forward to meeting our child.'

She laughs. 'Don't be ridiculous, Rupe! I had an abortion.'

I end the call. Think I'll finish the bottle of absinthe. It tastes disgusting, and the green fairy on the label sneers at me.

The Eni Inside

R Lennard

The creature that used to be Laurence Anderson fussed with his bow tie as he gazed into the reflective surface of the window overlooking the school grounds. He patted away the moisture on his mostly bald head with a cloth that he pulled from his pocket, nodded with satisfaction, then glared at the liver spots on his scalp as they pulsed with a bright purple light.

Slowly the glow faded. He stared harder at his reflection, looking for anything out of place. Absently, he wiped away the trickle of blood dripping from his nose. Rechecking his reflection in the window, he nodded and stepped closer to look at the unsuspecting children walking into the grounds of Ridden Hall.

He zeroed in on a gaggle of girls, eyes narrowing

as he tried to discern their Innarn abilities. There was one whose Innarn buzzed close to her skin. Now and then it would flare up, beautifully Dark and reeking of his home. She was the one who held the attention of the others. She would be the perfect target.

Eyes flicking back to his reflection again, he flinched. Laurence Anderson's last moments were the one clear memory he'd taken with him. The bark of the tree scraping his back even though the thick armour, the terror as the large bug with oversized mandibles had clambered into his mouth and pricked his tongue, paralysing him. The thick taste of fear and snot as the Eni had ripped apart his sinuses and forced itself into his brain, devouring memories in the limited time it had before it was discovered. The deepening ash and his grinning double his last view before he slipped from life.

It had taken months for Eni Anderson to be comfortable in this body. Attacking the host was not the way the Eni usually worked, but desperate times called for drastic measures. When the Wikkur had burnt down the forest which had been their home on Vennph, he'd needed a new host and by fluke, had found one who not only took pride in shaping the minds of the next generation on Ronah, but had heard whispers of the Altoriae as well. He'd been fortunate indeed, and now it was time to share his good fortune around.

The shark-like smile was out of place on the old

man's face as he contemplated the best way to introduce his brethren to the students of Ridden Hall.

Lissae shuddered as a call to the Dark Realms went out, droning on and on. She tried to pinpoint the call, but with millions of beings calling her home, it was a difficult job. She narrowed the call to the youngest of her Shifting Islands and sent the request for Ronah dealt with the problem. It was probably the Custodian anyway. With a deep sigh, the Realm went back to her regular business and ignored the call to Vennph.

The door to his office swung open, revealing his perfect target smiling at him, smoothing down her ridiculous skirt as she came into the room. 'You wanted to see me, Headmaster Anderson?' she asked.

'Yes, yes. Take a seat, Miss Thorne,' he said, gesturing to the extraordinary chair opposite him. The chair currently housed one of his many brothers, ready to read the insipid girls' thoughts.

She sat on the edge of the seat, twisting the hem of her skirt in her fingers. Eni Anderson had to admit he enjoyed eeking out the tension by staring at her over steepled fingers until a sheen of sweat coated her forehead.

'Let me be blunt with you, Miss Thorne. Your teachers have all approached me regarding you. It seems there is a great deal of disparity between your school work and your test results,' he said, careful to make his tone solemn. Eni Anderson had been unaware humans could turn grey, but he was still learning about the species.

The girl stuttered out an answer, and the creature felt the exact moment his brother was able to slide into her disjointed thoughts. He held up a hand to stop her.

'I care not about your reasoning, Miss Thorne, but know this,' he leant forward and the girl copied his movement, almost slipping from her seat. 'I see no need to worry when you have the highest test marks in your class.'

The girl sank back in her seat, turning white then red in quick succession. Eni Anderson hadn't known humans could do that either and idly wondered if it was because of his brother's scan.

'Between you and me, the Elders are looking for the Altoriae, and I think I've found her,' he tapped the side of his nose.

The girl looked at him and blinked, mouth agape. 'Who?' she breathed.

Eni Anderson grinned and leaned closer. 'You.'

Eyes widening momentarily, the girl smirked at him. 'I trust you won't say anything?' she said.

'Of course not. Keep up the good work, Miss Thorne,' he replied.

She nodded and rose on unsteady feet. 'Thank you, Headmaster,' she said and wobbled her way out of his office on heels too high.

'Were you able to create a link, brother?' Eni

Anderson sent telepathically. It would look rather odd if he were discovered talking to a chair.

'I was. The girl is not for us, another has claimed her,' his brother said as he made his way forward, clicking his mandibles in delight of being in his own form.

Eni Anderson felt his eyes narrow, and identified confusion and a healthy dose of fear from his brother. *'Fine. We will find another to be your host,'* he grumbled. A knock at the door had his brother turning back into the chair, and the next target entering the room.

It took only three days for forty hosts to be found, just enough for his surviving siblings. Eni Anderson felt like he had interviewed every child in the school and was still no closer to finding the Altoriae. Oh, there were plenty of unusual children on this hunk of moving rock, but none had exhibited the power or tenacity he expected of Lissae's greatest General.

He still had nine children to interview, more for the sake of disguising what he and his brethren were doing than anything else. These nine were either total non-Innarni or rated so low on their tests they barely warranted thinking about. Settling down for a tedious day, he suffered through the first eight interviews, and with a sigh, entreated the ninth to enter.

'Miss Dawn, isn't it? Have a seat,' Eni Anderson said, not bothering to watch as the child crossed the room to the chair. He missed the sharp look from the girl, the way she eyed the seat, and the deep breath she took before she affected a limp and slowly made her way to the desk.

'I'd best stand, headmaster. I fell and landed on my...' the girl said, and he finally raised his eyes as she indicated to her bruised rump.

'Ah. Well...' Eni Anderson said. One non-Innarni child who was missed by his brother was no loss to their cause.

How he would come to regret that errant thought.

The rest of the interview was stilted and just as dull as the other non-Innarni. Mentally, he marked her as one of the first to cull, and ended the discussion, his gaze fixed so firmly on the form of his brother, he missed the sad look and the lone tear which trailed down the girls' face as she silently slipped out the door.

'Have you no idea who the Altoriae is?' he sent to his brother.

'None. But there is delicious power on this island, ready for the taking,' his brother replied.

Eni Anderson sat back, pleased.

A week after the final interview, and the school hall was full of bodies, oddly silent as the children gazed up at their Headmaster. Eni Anderson was in his element, basking in the attention of so many gazes.

He'd created rows of seats which held his

hidden brethren, so when their chosen hosts sat down, they could start the process to learn their hosts' behaviours, and savour their memories before the shell was discarded and his brethren could take over.

Before the students could sit down, Eni Anderson felt the mental connection he'd always had with his brethren being severed, one link at a time, until only his brother in the chair upstairs remained.

In front of the crowded hall, the creature that used to be the Headmaster howled. Students who'd been about to sit down paused, confused and frightened, and the eldest acted, ushering everyone out of the room until there was only the howling Headmaster, a single child, and the Custodian left.

The girl stalked up to him, fire dancing in her eyes and plasma seeping from her fingertips. 'How many are left?' she gritted out, her clothes morphing into black war leathers, a blade appearing in her hand. If he'd been in his right mind, Eni Anderson would have laughed at the tiny girl looking up at him, her face scrunched into a furious countenance.

'Just one,' Eni Anderson sobbed. His whole family gone, bar one other. He couldn't lose them again. They were his everything. 'My brother. We are the last ones left.'

'The chair?' the Custodian asked softly, and the girl nodded, before his brother was Shifted from the Headmaster's office and into the hall where they stood in the blink of an eye.

Finally, Eni Anderson took notice. The tiny human before him was the Dawn girl, she had been the last child he'd interviewed - the one who'd refused to sit down. The liver-spots on his head glowed from inside as he struggled to dredge up a single memory of the girl from the original Laurence Anderson, and failed.

'Who are you?' he asked.

'Oh, don't be a fool,' said his brother as he shifted from his chair form and into an identical copy of the Custodian. The girl raised an eyebrow at his antics, but otherwise made no move. 'Clearly, this is the Altoriae the Elders have been harping on about.'

'Why did you come here?' the girl asked.

'So we could start again,' Eni Anderson answered.

'Don't tell her anything,' Eni Custodian hissed, striding around far too confidently to be the original. The Custodian was powerful, but far from arrogant. His brother thought he had the upper hand, though, and loved to show it when he could. He circled behind the girl, favoured twisted blade appearing in his hand.

She still didn't flinch. The creature could see the girl's lack of fear was enraging his brother, but he didn't know how to warn her - or him - not to do anything rash. Before he could form the words, his brother struck, attempting to stab the girl with his blade.

Dodging the blow, she countered with a jet of purple flames which poured from her hands and hit his brother's chest, sending him staggering back. Snarling, his brother slashed a hand through the air, and her plasma dissipated, drawn into the miniature thunderstorm his brother was creating. She laughed and grabbed the lightning as it streaked towards her, flinging it away from her and straight at the creature who'd taken the Headmaster's place.

The last thing Eni Anderson saw was the purple glow of plasma fuelled lightning streaking towards him, the sound of his brother's howl in his ears as his form collapsed, leaving behind the smoking clothes he'd so carefully picked out that morning.

His brother, when he joined him minutes later, told him the girl had wept, but it hadn't stopped her from flinging the same lightning at him, sending him from Lissae and into the Realm of the ghosts. Slowly, his brethren crowded around him, and the Eni were once again a family, content for the first time in millennia.

Nice Guy

Delia Strange

Apologies tumble out of her mouth in short pulses, like maple syrup glugging out of a bottle. Overly sweet platitudes wash over me, messy and sticky with half-truths and denial. Her face lowers before she peeks up through designer lashes; her expression intended less for my heart than my cock. It doesn't matter which she appeals to; I feel nothing.

No. Not nothing. Disgust. It heats my face. My upper lip is controlled by a masterful puppeteer. It twitches and lifts and feels bestial, like I'm a dog or bear or monster. She has brought out my worst, but my newfound awareness allows me clarity.

She has done it before. She will do it again. Dangling promises before me like the proverbial carrot, baiting me with smiles and tinkling laughter that I once thought innocent. She is no ingénue, she is as experienced as Babylon the Great. What I once read as a demure blush I now understand as the flush of excitement.

She betrayed me with her deception. I invested time and emotion into her, patiently waiting for her interest to grow. Every interaction between us is tainted now as I wonder; was I part of a routine? A result of careful tweaking? She has no love for me; I am a convenience, an accessory. I am the man who provides her a glamorous outing. I have become the sum of my parts; a nice house, a nice car, a nice face, a nice guy.

I'm sure she has other men; bad boys on bikes or philosophical poets. I don't have details, only the one I met; the married one. He is the same as her—worse! His gaze slithering over her as his wife kissed her cheek on the way to their table. The innuendo that passed between them and the laughter that followed. His wife pretends not to realise. But I don't.

I was right to stay calm, to finish the meal, to walk her to the carpark. I was also right to question her because her shock tells me all I need to know. At first her excuses come, dismissive and rehearsed. It is only when I pin her to my car that she understands I won't be fooled anymore. She finally admits his interest in her and qualifies they haven't slept together.

Of course they haven't. This is what she does—she makes promises she never fulfils; each smile, look or touch never ends in satisfaction. It's part of her game, devised to get whatever she wants, whenever she wants it. She is the modern woman; selfish and high on power. Hiding behind the mask of liberalism so she can justify using men like me for sport or prizes.

Tonight, her promise to me will be fulfilled. I will see to it.

The Australian Pen Series
COLLECT THE SET

Obliquity
Seventeen twisting tales of personal agendas, ulterior motives and surprise endings.

Futurevision
Twenty predictions about the future by twenty Australian authors

The Evil Inside Us
Twenty-two tales revealing our worst secrets and our darkest fears.

Available at all leading book retailers

Femme: Light

Is love real when it's an obligation?

Kaley Blackburn is invited to the world of Femme representing her university. She knew about its culture of slavery but didn't think she'd have to participate... until a man is assigned to serve her.

Mecca is a thoughtful and informative guide to the futuristic utopia that is his home. But as Kaley digs deeper, she discovers the world of Femme is only beautiful on the surface.

Femme: Light by Delia Strange is an explorative journey into the *Wanderer* multiverse. The novel has a definitive ending, a single perspective and hints of political undercurrents set in a technologically advanced world.

Read *Femme: Light* for a quick dip into a world of role-reversal.

Available at all leading book retailers

www.ingramcontent.com/pod-product-compliance
Lightning Source LLC
Chambersburg PA
CBHW021432110726
47901CB00008B/2392